Astro Saga

ROBERT SMITHBURY
email: astro.saga.oblique.media@gmail.com

The Celestial Secrets
Part IV

ROBERT SMITHBURY
email: astro.saga.oblique.media@gmail.com

*The Fourth Secret
Published by Oblique Media Group Ltd.*

*Other books by Robert Smithbury also published by
Oblique Media*

ASTRO SAGA

The Celestial Secrets

The First Secret
The Second Secret
The Third Secret
The Fifth Secret
The Sixth Secret
The Seventh and Final Secrets

The Fourth Secret

by

Robert Smithbury

ROBERT SMITHBURY
email: astro.saga.oblique.media@gmail.com

To Eden, for being so patient

Contents

Living in an asteroid 8
Maps of the inhabited asteroids in earth orbit 12
Prologue: The fallen egg 16
Chapter 1: Pirates? 28
Chapter 2: Visitors! 37
Chapter 3: Hot dogs 49
Chapter 4: Kidnapped! 63
Chapter 5: Guess who 78
Chapter 6: Dragon! 90
Chapter 7: Eruption 99
Chapter 8: From the frying pan… 107
Chapter 9: Mush! 114
Chapter 10: Riding the thunderstorm 121
Chapter 11: …into the fire 131
Chapter 12: If auld acquaintance be forgot… 142
Chapter 13: A cunning plan 153
Chapter 14: Snatching an egg from the furnace 163
Chapter 15: Falling 175

ROBERT SMITHBURY
email: astro.saga.oblique.media@gmail.com

Living in an asteroid

Following a cataclysm several centuries ago humanity abandoned Earth. The alternative was to face extinction and therefore they were compelled to find somewhere else to live.

The other planets around our sun are inhospitable places and therefore new habitats had to be manufactured. The asteroids were identified as being able to provide ample raw materials but were unfortunately too far from the Sun to be viable. Over a period of several years, suitable asteroids were towed into safe areas of Earth's orbit and aligned in five layers around the Sun.

The process of converting these into habitable environments then began, but time and materials were beginning to run out. As a result most of the asteroids were initially fitted out with only minimal facilities and the addition of customised environments following later. In many instances this has enabled individual communities to configure the layout of the interiors to meet their own cultural ideals. Consequently, there is significant diversity in the style of habitats amongst the current Astro-Nations.

In some areas the inequalities in the distribution of resources has led to local depravation, rising tension and conflict.

Asteroid habitats tend to follow a common design, dictated by the availability of time and resources available at the time of their construction. This involves a hollowed out interior that is then set spinning to create an artificial gravity inside. Communities were laid out on the inside of the exterior shell of the asteroids.

In the majority of designs attempts have been made to create artificial skies along the axis of the asteroid's spin. These have been only partially effective and in most asteroids it is still possible to see the communities on the opposite interior suspended kilometres above the artificial sky. This has led to a decrease in the mental health of some citizens and Astro-Nations report higher health cost ratios post migration compared to the levels experienced on Earth.

The hurried timetable for the fit out of some asteroids has led to a number of subsequent catastrophes arising from poor design and the maintenance of adequate records related to the construction. The worst of these was New Attica in 2297 when a gunshot fractured a thin section of the asteroid's shell leading to a major disaster as the artificial atmosphere dissipated in less than an hour. Official casualty figures of 3,757,293 fatalities were recorded but some agencies consider these to be under estimates. New Attica has only recently completed its re-population programme.

THE FOURTH SECRET
email: astro.saga.oblique.media@gmail.com

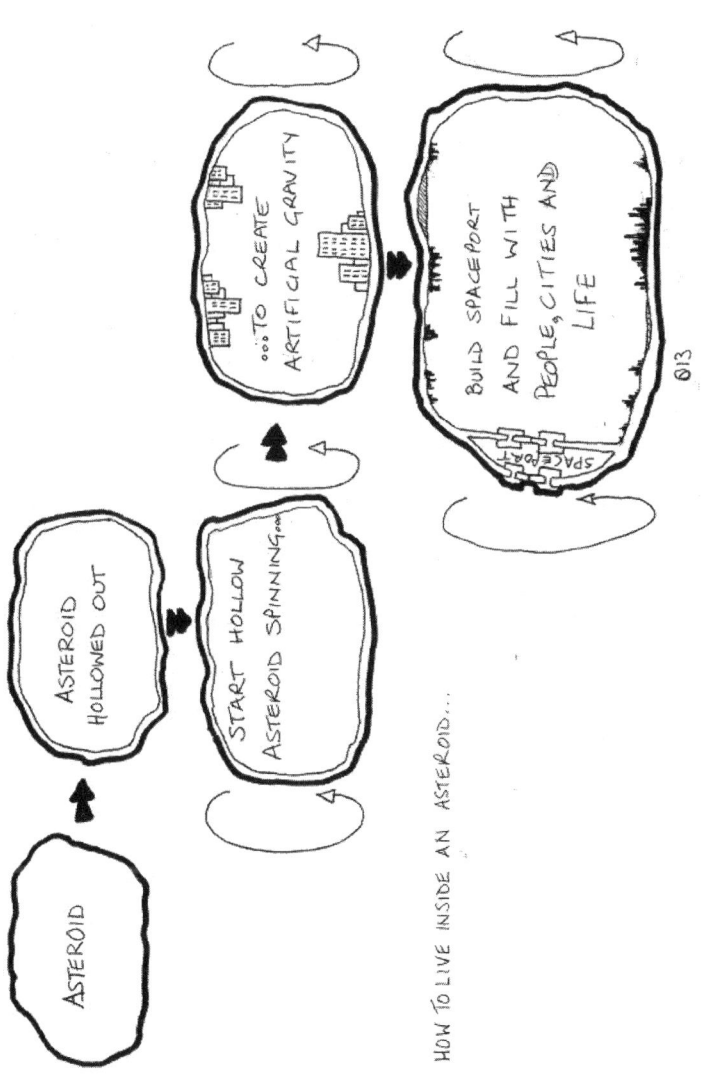

ROBERT SMITHBURY
email: astro.saga.oblique.media@gmail.com

Maps of the inhabited asteroids in earth orbit

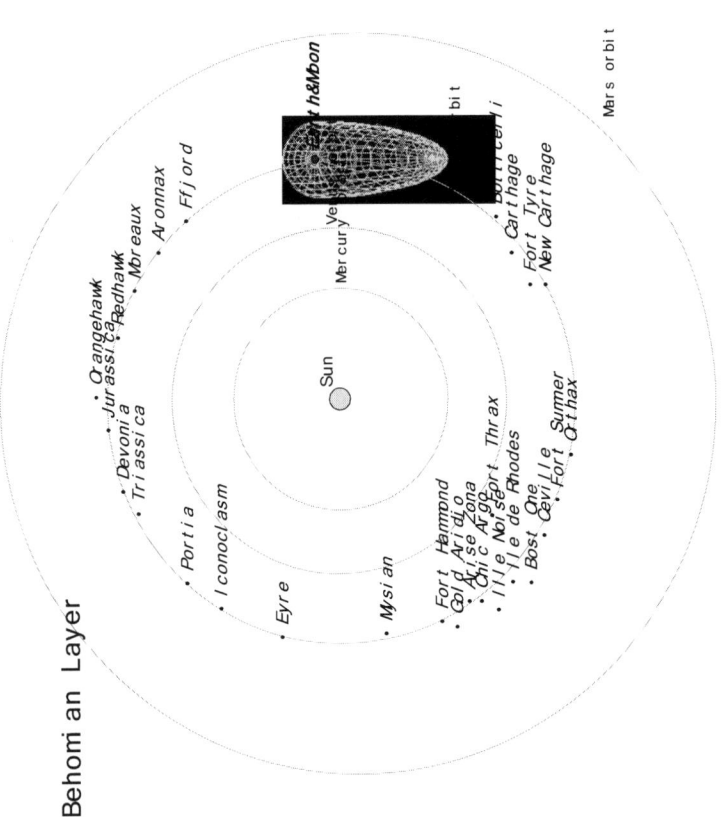

The majority of the action in the Fourth Secret takes place inside the Triassica asteroid. The Triassica asteroid orbits in the Behomian layer of asteroids, (see below).

THE FOURTH SECRET
email: astro.saga.oblique.media@gmail.com

The Behomian Layer of Asteroids is one of five layers of asteroids orbiting the earth. It aligns with the Tropic of Cancer.

The heroes of this saga have so far visited two other layers: the Midgard and Retovian layers, which align with the Equator and Tropic of Capricorn respectively.

The other two maps are replicated below.

ROBERT SMITHBURY
email: astro.saga.oblique.media@gmail.com

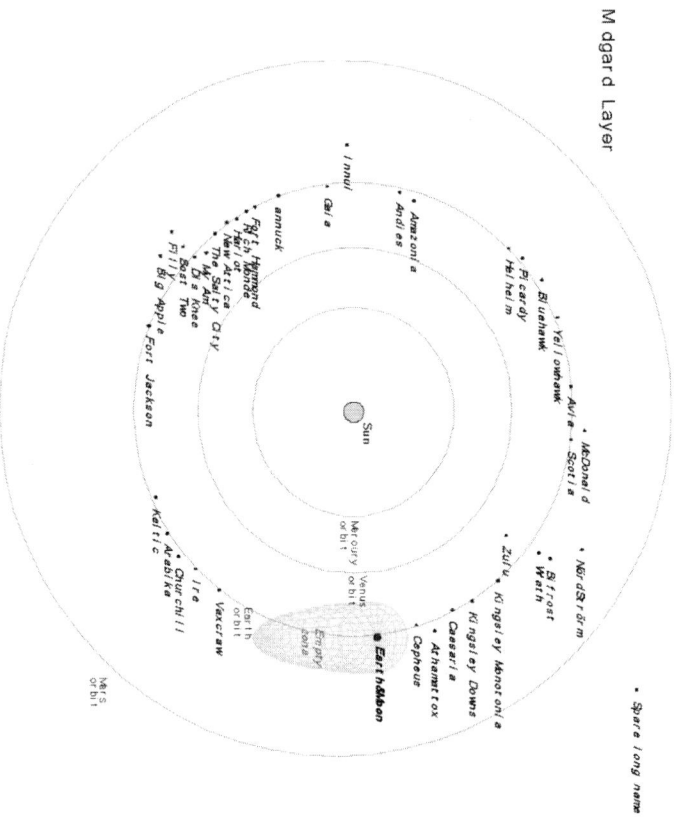

THE FOURTH SECRET
email: astro.saga.oblique.media@gmail.com

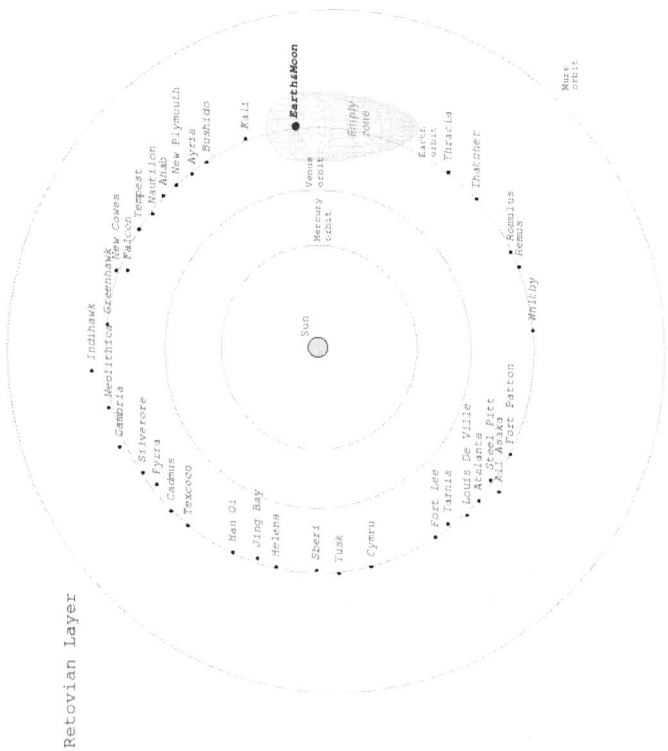

Prologue: The fallen egg

Tina, a Tyrannosaurus Rex, was temporarily ignoring the recent tremors beneath her huge hind claws. Instead, she stared up at the strange object that hurtled across the night sky on a trajectory straight towards her and her nest.

It burned a bright and angry blue, far more vivid than the long, aching, sulphurous glow of the volcanoes that belched continuous smoke and fire. This new celestial object potentially represented something much more dangerous and deadly, drawing a heavy line of distress in her direction. But that's for later.

With delicate sensitivity that was totally at odds with her ferocious expression, rows of razor sharp teeth and her enormous size she checked once more on her clutch of eggs and continued fretting. She'd deliberately set her nest up within this small cave to avoid the danger from meteor strikes. She'd done the best she could to protect them, and now this.

Unfortunately, she didn't have time to move any of them now. It looked like she was about to find out if she'd done enough. She'd just have to hope that they'd be okay. Being an expectant mother wasn't easy and maternal anxiety didn't sit comfortably with the T-Rex's normal sentiment of ferocity and all round bad-cussedness.

With a poorly disguised sense of emergency, she crooned and cooed at them, gently nuzzling them closer together, covering them under her huge bulk. It was a vain attempt to shelter them from the impact of the flying object. You could never tell. Inwardly she tensed her muscles and winced. This might hurt. Closing her eyes tightly she waited for the impact.

With an angry groan, the ground shook violently and a heavy shower of dirt sprayed across her. Roaring, she climbed precariously to her feet and staggered out onto the open ground in front of the cave.

Deep rooted, reverberating roars are the traditional way to deal with most problems if you're a T-Rex. Shouting also usually works as well. If not, throw in some ground stomping and a bit of charging. So far, it had worked every time for Tina.

After a couple more deep throated growls, she felt ready to face any impending danger with 100 tonnes of sinew, muscle and armour backed up by bone crushing jaws and cruel claws. When you're built like that it does amazing things to your self impressions of importance and invulnerability. You don't often meet a self-conscious, shy T-Rex and Tina definitely wasn't one of them.

Of course, whilst the body of a T Rex is huge and impressive, its brain is small and stupid. Hence the reason humans had grown Tina from a chain of dinosaur DNA and not the other way around. If dinosaurs had more brains, perhaps they'd be growing humans in their laboratories.

For Tina, growling, roaring, alert and ready to tear something, anything, to pieces for covering her with dirt, there was just one problem. There was no one there.

The space outside of the cave was totally devoid of life, as normal.

But something was different.

The landscape?

Yes, the landscape.

The ground now seemed to rear up in front of her, where before it had been flat. Yes, she was sure of it. There was a moderate ridge where before there had only been arid, flat, dirt surrounded by high-sided cliffs towering over a long, thin valley, covered in bones.

On the other side of this new ridge, a fire flared into life with thick, black smoke disappearing into the

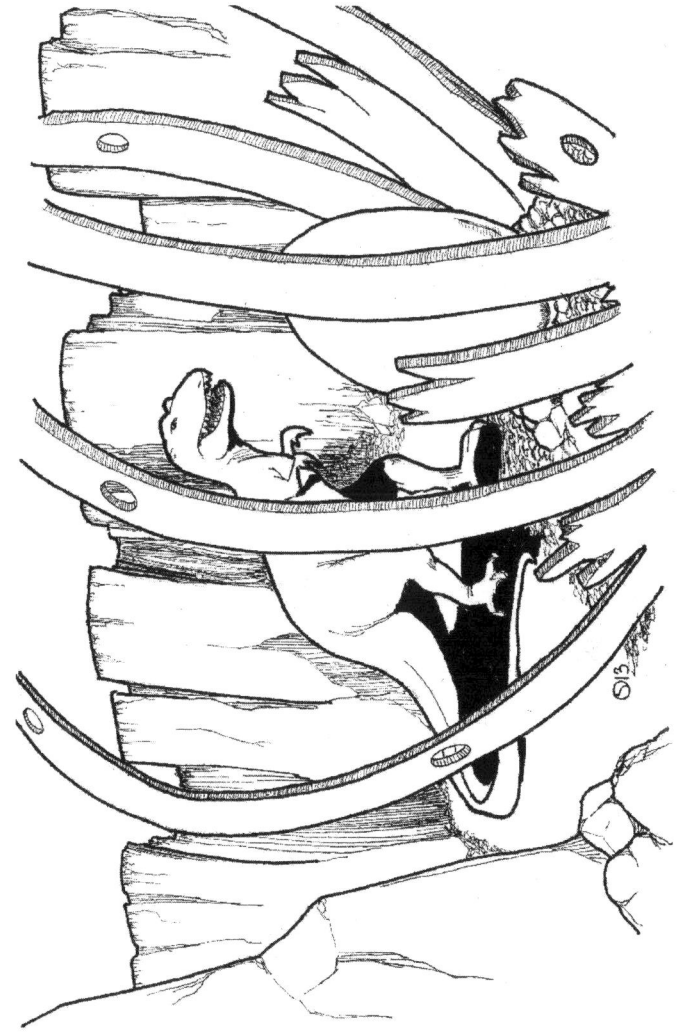

darkening dusk. The mother inside her hoped that the

fire wouldn't spread. If it did, then she'd have to move her nest away quickly. Much easier said than done for a dinosaur with only residual forearms and a bite that could tear through an armoured pressure dome like wet tissue paper.

She growled low in her throat, mostly out of habit, but also from general dissatisfaction with her life. There was no alternative. She'd have to go and check out the fire and see if it was likely to spread. Calling for her mate, Timothy, to watch carefully over her eggs whilst she was away, she hurried around the edge of the crater.

Cresting the ridge, she gazed down into the impact site of tangled and twisted metal. She was in luck; the fire was already showing signs of going out. Tentatively she poked around disinterestedly at some of the smouldering wreckage.

Looking more closely, she could see that a human lay amidst the smoking debris. Her heart fluttered with panic for a moment. Was this a hunter's trap? Was he lying there in wait to satisfy her curiosity with a pointed, poisonous death?

No, he was clearly dead. The bottom part of his torso was missing and that bright red liquid that they were filled with was oozing out onto the dirt.

It was then that she saw something that made her own blood boil and set her nerve endings alight with rage. In his outstretched hands, he held an egg.

One of her eggs? It had to be. Where else would an egg come from here?

Hurrying to the scene before the egg became cold, she gently nudged it up the slope with her nose, trampling the fallen spaceman into a forgotten grave as she did. At the top, it rolled easily down the other side and she 'returned' it to her nest as quickly as she could.

Temporary relief flooded through her. All mothers have an in-built anxiety about their eggs. The fire flickered its last and Tina settled herself back into position.

Unfortunately, this momentary respite from a life of fretful stress wasn't to last. The soft sound of slowly beating wings advancing down the valley and slid into her consciousness. What now?

Twitching her thick neck backwards and forwards, searching the sky, she spotted the source of the annoying noise. A yellow dragon and its rider circled high above them, back lit by the remnants of the day, clinging to the sky against the sudden, encroaching storm.

She roared at it loudly for effect. Unless the rider was a hunter then they were in no danger from a single yellow dragon. Not even a sole black dragon would concern her. A thousand yellows or a dozen blacks maybe, but a single puny yellow one wouldn't be any threat to her and her clutch.

The rider was unlikely to be a hunter anyway. It was too far away. Hunters usually wanted to experience the risk of being up close to the kill on something as symbolic as a T-Rex. Shooting a Tyrannosaurus from the back of a yellow dragon circling high overhead was unlikely to be considered 'sporting'. It was far more 'honourable', for hunters to place themselves within charging distance, apparently. There was something exciting about felling a charging T-Rex as it thundered towards you. Bringing it crashing to the ground within touching distance of where you stood. Evidently that was 'honourable heroism'.

From close range there was less risk of the hunter's shot missing and breaking through the thick skin of the asteroid. Neither Tina, nor Timothy knew anything about the Celestial physics of asteroid habitation. They had absolutely no understanding of the thousand technical miracles that it took to create their special volcanic habitat inside the asteroid of Triassica. The hunters knew though and that was all that mattered. Supposedly something about self-preservation.

Personally, Tina didn't spare a lot of time for more advanced thinking and philosophy. Kill, eat, belch, sleep, kill eat, etc. etc. made much more sense.

She took one last hungry look at the circling dragon. Just let it come within reach and she'd dine on dragon wings for supper. Her stomach growled in hungry agreement. Fresh dragon wings were scrummy.

~o0o~

In close orbit alongside to the asteroid of Arronax was the Aztex Battle Cruiser, 'The Soul of the Conqueror'. Its commander, Lord Steal, agreed to take the urgent message from the Triassica dragon scout unit directly from his position on the bridge.

"Lord Steal, it is my extreme pleasure to inform you that we have tracked down one of the surviving mini ships from the Typhon. You were correct, it appears to have entered Triassica. Unfortunately, it crash landed in the Dinosaur park at Saurox before we could safely transfer off the Celestial Secret that was undoubtedly on board."

Lord Steal beamed with pride. He loved being right and even more so when someone else noticed it. He also felt elated that the Fourth Celestial Secret was almost within his grasp. Whilst the first three had eluded him by some unlucky and strange combination of luck and fate, the fourth would surely be his. He was so wrapped up in feeling delighted about his impending victory that he almost didn't hear what the scout said next.

"...crash landed and all of the occupants are confirmed dead. The Celestial Secret now appears to be in the possession of a pair of Tyrannosaurus Rex."

"Curses!" muttered Lord Steal, darkly. His thick brows knitted together and his grisly beard squirmed disgustingly.

"Well don't just stay there flapping your wings. Go down and get it off of them, you fool!" thundered Lord Steal in an uncharacteristic moment of weakness and compassion.

The scout quailed, "But…my lord…." he wailed.

"You have your orders!" raged Lord Steal. "Or do I have to think of another particularly unpleasant punishment that would be far more horrifying than unarmed wrestling with a ferocious dinosaur!"

There was only silence on the other end as far away, inside Triassica, the petrified dragon and rider circled lower. Eager eyed, the solider leaned as far forwards as he could. He gulped. If he could avoid a direct confrontation with the dinosaurs that would be preferable but at the moment he couldn't see anyway of recovering the Celestial Secret without going in and taking it.

Perhaps if he sneaked in whilst the dinosaur was looking the other way. That might work...

Lower and lower they glided.

Closer and closer, thought Tina as she looked the other way whilst simultaneously watching the dragon's descending shadow.

Just a little bit closer.

Lord Steal paced the bridge silently, waiting for news of success.

It came within a few minutes, but not in the way he had hoped.

"I'm afraid that we've lost contact with the yellow dragon scout," reported back the communications officer. "The signal has gone dead at the other end. It may just be a technical problem; the local weather's playing havoc with the gadgetry... but...."

Lord Steal raged in silence for more than a few microseconds during which time some of the junior officers on the bridge were sure that they could see steam coming out of his ears, or maybe his wiry beard was smouldering.

"I want our best flight of black dragons retrained for combat with T-Rex," he thundered. "I will create a black squadron that will recover the Celestial Secret stolen by those... those test tube reptiles!"

He paused for dramatic effect.

"Set a course for Triassica!"

"Aye, aye, Lord Steal."

Whilst the mighty warship accelerated across the solar system, the diminutive tyrant pondered and plotted, pounding his fists on the arm of the chair as he did so. He would create the most fearsome fighting force in the solar system, Lord Steal's Black Dragons!

He smiled an evil grin. He quite liked the sound of that but then he tended to like any title that had his name in it. And even if it didn't work it was such a cool sounding name that he could surely turn it into a successful business.

It was agreed then. This was a good plan!

~oOo~

Deep inside Triassica, Tina and Timothy enjoyed a good supper of fresh yellow dragon wings with a side order of ribs. It tasted good. So good that Timothy made a mental note to look out for another chance to try dragon and human sandwiches again.

Maybe more barbecue sauce next time?

ROBERT SMITHBURY
email: astro.saga.oblique.media@gmail.com

Chapter 1: Pirates?

Torr was woken by the clamouring of klaxon alarms going off across his spaceship, the Eos. He leapt out of bed and half dressed, headed for the bridge.

Stumbling half naked into the room he jumped back behind the door as he realised that Nattie and Fuzz ball were already there ahead of him. They were the remaining, both female, members of the crew, (as long as you ignored Kiki, the slightly annoying, kid-friendly computer). Struggling into the rest of his clothes he edged back onto the bridge hoping that no one had noticed him previously. He was in luck.

"Kiki, cut the alarms out and tell me what all of the noise is about!" he shouted above the noise.

"Pirate attack!" announced the onboard computer with an arrogant personality overlay that was seriously too much for so early in the morning.

If you're a computer who doesn't need to sleep then you can get out of synch with your human companions.

At the word 'Pirate', the three of them instinctively ducked below the viewing ports.

"Pirates?!"

"Where?"

"About 35 degrees to port and slightly sunward of us. There's a tourist ship that appears to be under attack by ... Well, you should take a look for yourself."

Kiki displayed an image of a small, but rather bloated ship sitting motionless against a backdrop of stars surrounded by a fantastical display of exploding lights bouncing off its crumbling shields. It looked like a perfect image of vulnerability. Impossibly from above, a much larger dragon shape swept through space on giant wings. Torr's mind boggled at the sight, struggling to make sense of the talons outstretched towards the smaller ship.

But Torr was getting used to dealing with the unusual and slightly surprising.

"Kiki, arm the Ionic cannons! Everyone, battle stations!"

"Battle stations? Battle stations? Where are our battle stations? No one has ever mentioned battle stations before. Have we discussed this? I don't recall discussing this."

"Nattie, shut up and get your space suit on."

Nattie glared at him and gave him a look that said, 'I'm going to have words to say about this later,' but did what he asked.

Fuzz ball, as usual, bumbled about cutely and tried not to get in the way whilst achieving totally, absolutely nothing.

The Eos accelerated with a lurch and swept forwards.

Torr was feeling grumpy; he had a thing about being woken by loud noises. It was going to feel good to take his foul mood out on some bad guys. He grabbed the controls of the ship's gunnery systems and sighted in on the swooping dragon. How was a dragon able to live in space anyway? He'd be doing reality a service.

Ignoring the question that continued to kick around at the back of his brain, he thumbed off the safety controls. If he could live knowing about space aliens, underwater monsters and evil empires he was sure it wouldn't hurt him to suspend disbelief long enough to deal with an extraterrestrial flying lizard, a random improbability field, or something equally unbelievable.

"Kiki, give me full manual control," Torr commanded, releasing the safety catches.

"Torr, I don't think that's wise."

"I'm not asking you to think. Just do it."

If it was possible for a computer to sigh, Kiki sighed.

Once he'd felt the comforting tremor of the manual controls being handed over, Torr promptly sighted and fired, twice. There were two low thuds and a jolt before a couple of streaming lines of light burst from the sides of the Eos and raced across space towards their target.

In response, the dragon impossibly reversed direction and swept itself out of the line of fire. Instead, the two shots caught the space ship that was under attack with glancing blows and small blasts. There were detonations amidships that exploded in expanding balls of flame.

Torr had missed the dragon and hit the space ship instead.

"Stop! Stop! Why are you attacking us?" screamed a whining voice over the speakers.

Torr was speechless and stood there, open mouthed, at the controls. Nattie marched across and thumbed the safety catches back on again.

"Oh, well done! That was just sooo clever."

She switched on the communications channel.

"I'm very sorry, but there appears to have been some form of mistake. We were trying to hit the dragon that was attacking you."

"They're not attacking us! We're a tourist ship from Triassica and the 'pirate attack' is just a part of the show that we put on for our guests. It's not a real dragon, it's a dragon shaped spaceship, you fools! How could a real dragon live in space? It's just a spaceship called the Dragon's Storm."

Nattie glared at Torr, "Battle stations indeed…" she hissed quietly.

Torr looked away. His face was burning with embarrassment. But Kiki had said that the space ship was under attack!

"Well, you've damaged us now and we need to off board some passengers. Since you're the ones that have caused all of the trouble the least you could do is ferry some of our passengers back inside the asteroid whilst we make repairs."

"Of course," muttered Nattie, humiliated. "Kiki, please take us alongside and prepare to take on passengers."

~oOo~

A little later the three space ships were nestled together and Nattie, Fuzz ball along with a very reluctant, silent, Torr were onboard the Santa Anna, which was the name of the ship that they had thought was under attack. Everyone on board wore space suits while the crew struggled to restore air pressure in the damaged sections.

To Torr's dismay, Nattie had agreed to take seven passengers on board the Eos for transport to the inside of Triassica. Even worse, they were all young girls who seemed to have nothing better to do than point and giggle. His day was getting steadily worse.

On the plus side, there appeared to be an interesting conversation going on between the Captain of the Santa Anna and the Captain of the Dragon's Storm. The Captain of the dragon ship was a big, imposing woman in what could only be described as a wildly flamboyant space suit. Covered in crimson and white feathers, her thin legs poked out from a flurry of fluff, reminding him of a giant flamingo.

Torr nonchalantly tried to edge closer so he could hear more of what they were talking about. He still had a niggling feeling that something wasn't quite right here. Kiki had said there were pirates and whilst he was usually incredibly annoying he was also seldom wrong.

Torr could only make out small phrases of their conversation.

"...did you invite them on board..."

"...up appearances..."

"...ransomed them all..."

What were they talking about? Were the two captains conspiring in some fiendish plot together? Or was Torr just jumping to the wrong conclusions again? He didn't know anymore. He was confused and he already felt like a fool. Perhaps he was going mad. He'd heard that obscure fascinations with possible alien conspiracies could do that to you.

He tried to hide by edging behind Nattie before the Captain of the Dragon's Storm noticed him listening to her conversation. But he was too late, he'd already captured her attention.

"Hello my dears!" she simpered as she waddled up to them on those unfashionably long legs and wound her arms around their shoulders in an unnecessarily camaraderie fashion.

Fuzz ball tried to hide between their legs as the woman's voice boomed out in a commanding fashion.

"My name is Lady Lucretia Medea. I see you've caused a bit of a stir here. Never mind, I'm sure it can all be sorted out. Now, since these poor people don't have a working space ship anymore, if you would be so kind as to escort our guests to the Saurox Theme Park inside Triassica I'm sure that we can forget about the whole thing."

She smiled a false smile at them and hugged her hands together.

There must be millions of astrodollars worth of damage here, fretted Nattie suspiciously. Why were they so willing to ignore it and who was this weird woman to go around making these sort of promises? Nattie's suspicions were heading in the same direction as Torr's.

Medea, Medea? thought Torr. Where had he heard that name before? In buried memories of half finished stories, myths and deep, dark legends?

There was no use denying it any longer, both of their suspicions were aroused.

THE FOURTH SECRET
email: astro.saga.oblique.media@gmail.com

Chapter 2: Visitors!

Back aboard the Eos, Torr locked himself in his bedroom and left Nattie to giggle away with their new 'passengers'. The first three were quite unsettling. They were Kara, Sara and Tara Blaine, who were triplets with the really annoying habit of completing each other's sentences. The remaining four girls were all reassuringly different, but to Torr's mind just as annoying. Their names were Holly Weir, Sophia Ling, Sammy O'Reilly and Ubie Ozara, who all claimed to be 'dearest' friends to the triplets.

All seven of them appeared to be incurably excited about being onboard without any adults. To Torr's further dismay they seemed to have brought an endless supply of conversation and baggage with them. On the other hand, Fuzz ball was in her element as all of the girls wanted to stroke and hug her at once. The whole thing was driving Torr crazy.

Nattie was elated. Not only had she just acquired a whole group of new friends, but her theories about Kiki's ability to expand the Eos to accommodate more occupants had now been proved as well. Whilst she couldn't put her finger on exactly what he'd done, there were clearly new rooms for all of their recently arrived guests. What she couldn't figure out, though, was why the rooms all looked like they always had been there. They even had dust, dirty fingerprints and a 'lived in' smell. How did that happen?

Her curiosity was piqued and it always liked a mystery. She loved a challenge.

In the relative quiet of his room, Torr was thinking about their situation and what the events of the last few hours meant. He was trying to balance out the good things with the bad.

They were heading towards Triassica. That was a good sign. Kiki had told them that at least one of the remaining Celestial Secrets was heading in the same direction. That was another good sign. The Saurox dinosaur theme park sounded kind of interesting as well. That was another one. There were definitely some plus sides to his situation.

On the downside, he was on a space ship with eight girls and Fuzz ball. That wasn't so good. Three of the girls looked identical, which troubled him. Torr wasn't good with girls. He could just about deal with Nattie and Fuzz ball didn't really count. Identical girls were a bit freaky. Just what was the difference between identical triplets and clones?

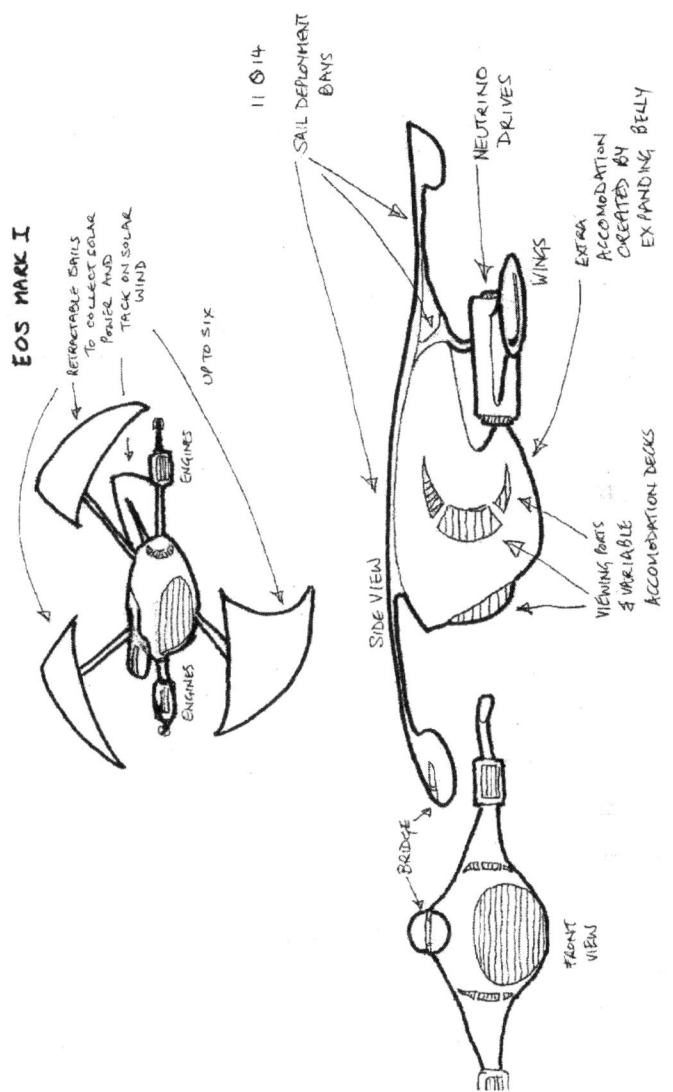

He turned his attention back to more important matters. Three Celestial Secrets had already been safely recovered. He'd discovered that his parents had disappeared near a black hole. One of the remaining secrets controlled black holes, preventing them from wandering into inhabited space. Was there a connection?

He wondered whether he could use one of the remaining Celestial Secrets to help him find his parents or, indeed, whether the Tinkerer would let him. They weren't supposed to be used by individuals for their own benefit, they were meant to help all of humanity. It was the selfish actions of the Carthaginians and the Aztex Empire that had got mankind into this mess in the first place.

Torr didn't know the answer to any of these questions, but he vowed to find out. He was going to find his parents, whatever it took.

His deliberations were interrupted by a soft tapping on the door of his room.

"Torr, it's me," whispered Nattie. "Can I come in? It's alright, I'm alone."

He opened the door slowly but when he saw it really was only Nattie he quickly let her in and shut it firmly behind her.

"Are you OK?" she asked.

"Yeah, of course," he bluffed. "When you've taken on Lord Steal, Dr Wunderfoul, Professor Banx, death and the Nebulon III, a few girls aren't going to bother you."

"Yes, I know what you mean," she muttered, shaking her head. "At first I thought it would be nice to have a few different people on board, but I'm already beginning to regret it. I thought it would be like having Kezin back, but sadly it's not. Some of them aren't even very different."

"Hmm. I miss him too," Torr admitted reluctantly. "But you make a good substitute," he nudged her playfully in the ribs.

Nattie shoved him back and they spent the next few minutes reflecting on the adventures the two of them had been through together in pursuit of the first three Celestial Secrets; the Tinkerer and his wondrous inventions, the watery pollution of Nautilon; and the frozen wastes of Nordstrom. They debated fiercely whether the imaginary Merfolk really existed and shivered at their memorable encounter with the giant hunter-killer polar bears. They spoke mostly about their successes rather than the dangers that no doubt remained. It seemed safer that way.

There was no mention of the Aztex and Carthaginian spaceships that were no doubt still in pursuit of them. But however much they tried to focus on how successful they'd been they kept coming back to the same place. There were still four Celestial Secrets to find before humanity would be safe again and Torr would have a chance of being reunited with his parents. They were still less than half way through. There still seemed an awful lot to do.

They'd been tracking the nearest Celestial Secrets for several days now as it moved erratically through the asteroids circling the sun in earth's orbit. The asteroids orbited in five rough shaped rings, dragged into place by the human race in an attempt to provide enough living space when Earth became uninhabitable.

The existence of the Seven Celestial Secrets was unknown to the billions of humans scattered throughout the asteroids. Hardly anyone knew how vital they were for human survival without the Earth to protect them. Each egg shaped object contained alien technology that kept the human colonies safe. If the eggs were tampered with then they'd shut down with disastrous consequences for everyone.

Torr and Nattie had managed to recover three of them after outwitting the Aztex and Carthaginian Empires who were also after the secrets. Fortunately, the Tinkerer had now restored them to full working order after Zarrox, the Keeper of the Secrets, had sabotaged them to prevent their misuse. Now that the Tinkerer had safely returned them to their normal purpose Torr and Nattie no longer had to worry about the havoc that might arise should they fall into the wrong hands. But the other four were still out there, somewhere…

If they didn't succeed in their quest to recover them there was no telling how much danger the human race might be in. Whilst the Celestial Secrets provided mankind with much needed technology, they could also be used as powerful weapons that could bring humanity to its knees, or possibly push it into total extinction. Torr couldn't begin to comprehend how many lives might be lost if a black hole were to be directed through the heart of the heaviest populated areas of the asteroids. He just didn't want to think about it. Some things were just too scary to ponder for too long.

The speaker crackled, which was Kiki's equivalent of clearing his throat before saying something monumental.

"I have some good news," Kiki announced in his usual, crazy, ebullient way.

They waited patiently for him to continue. There was never any point in trying to hurry him. If you did it always ended up taking much longer. He almost sounded excited.

"The Fourth Celestial Secret has stopped moving. It's been stationery now for over twelve hours."

"Where it is Kiki?" asked Nattie, immediately interested.

"Triassica!" he announced triumphantly, almost as if he wanted to add 'I told you so'. "We just need to drop our passengers off and we can get on with recovering it."

Somehow, Torr didn't feel so triumphant. Recovering the Celestial Secrets was never as easy as just walking by and picking them up. There were bound to be hiccups and he was making painfully slow progress in finding his parents. His thoughts returned to the black hole they'd been in orbit around when they'd sent in their last report. How do you force a black hole to do what you want it to?

There were still too many unanswered questions for his liking. With the helpful finality of

Kiki's news, bringing a bleak certainty to what they needed to do next, he and Nattie said good night to each other.

~o0o~

Ahead of them, far away inside the asteroid of Triassica, six very real and very deadly black dragons were being put through their paces. They had been hatched only a few days previously and their assigned destiny was to become Lord Steal's black squadron of T-Rex fighting dragons.

Two of them, Fang and Midnight, were facing each other across the sawdust ring. Smoke rose and venom dripped as their horned rear claws dug deep into the ground. Red eyes burned deeply within horned eye sockets and with wings fully flared; they glared malevolently at each other.

Midnight's fore claw dug into the ground, leaving huge gashes and in response Fang bellowed a challenge. Midnight waited no longer and hurled himself at Fang's neck. His claws and teeth were outstretched and ready to bite something, anything that got in his way.

"I say," muttered Rip to Eclipse as they watched the other two dragons clash in a crescendo of sound. In front of them Fang collapsed to the ground amidst a flurry of claws. "Good show!"

Eclipse sniffed and ignored him. She didn't have much sympathy for anyone. Especially not for Fang's aggressive, bullying, over inflated ego. He deserved a beating.

Fang scrabbled frantically under Midnight's furious onslaught. Flailing around he panicked and grabbed for a something, anything, to assist him.

Soot, the tiniest of the Black Dragons yelped a pitiful cry that ascended into a full-bloodied scream. Fang's claws had grabbed the smaller dragon's ankle firmly and lifted him clear of the ground before swinging him around in a wide arc.

"Not on!" growled Rip. "Poor show."

"Shut your meat hole!" snarled Smasher. "All's fair in …"

But before he could finish he had to duck as Soot swung towards him. Moments later Fang was pounding poor Soot over Midnight's head in a vain attempt to free himself from the larger dragon's punishing grip. Midnight winced slightly, there was a moment's respite and Fang wriggled free.

"He started before I was ready!" Fang wailed, retreating across the sawdust ring with a hurried limp. "I could have beaten you in a fair fight. Just say the word and we'll go again, you big wuss!"

Midnight, of course, said nothing. He never did. Mute since birth, with a genetic flaw from being hatched too quickly, the largest of the Black Dragons just glared with haunted eyes at his protagonist.

Soot sat on his tail where he had landed 20 metres away, clutching at his nozzle, "My dose! I think you broke my dose," he started to sob.

"Oh for goodness sake," sighed Eclipse, heading back to their nests. "If we had brains we'd be dangerous."

~oOo~

Later, back aboard the Eos as Torr started to drift off to sleep, his mind continued to wander through his problems. Two lost parents, one black hole, four Celestial Secrets, eight irritating girls and a mysterious battle with some false pirates? Lots of numbers, but what did they add up to?

Chapter 3: Hot dogs

Torr woke from his dreams with a start. They'd been so real that he could still taste the tang of panic on his tongue.

He'd dreamt that he'd been riding a huge black dragon through a terrible electric storm. Overhead had loomed the impossible bulk of a Carthaginian Battle Cruiser far too close to the ground. They'd come in close around the towers of a spindly, tall castle. Bats flew everywhere. Fingers of fear tickled at his spine.

He had an awful dread of castles and Carthaginian Battle Cruisers. He could feel their eyes searching for him everywhere, seeking him with huge, unstoppable search beams.

Strangely the scene had shifted and somehow he was suddenly inside the castle. The room had been gloomily dark and bursts of lightening through the slit window were the only illumination. A large wooden table filled the centre of the circular room with arcane runes gouged into its surface. On the table was a book, ancient and enticing, compelling and terrifying.

In between searing flashes he'd tried to make out the title but met with only frustrating failure. Then in one particularly elongated phosphorescent pyrotechnic display he'd caught it, 'Myths and Legends of Black Holes', by Professor Erin Naydo.

His heart leapt and his fingers had grabbed for the book before it slipped away from him, hurling itself to the floor. He dived after it but it easily eluded him, heading for the door. Floor to door, floor to door, it mocked, whilst on the other side of the heavy, metal-set, wooden frame he heard footsteps. Heavy, inconclusive, footsteps pounding with the insane counter rhythm of a human heartbeat.

Someone was running. Running towards him from far away. Who was running towards him; friend or foe, clue or distraction, enemy or accomplice?

The footsteps reached the other side of the door. The handle had just started to turn before he'd woken with a certainty that something was about to go very badly wrong.

Then he realised it probably already had.

Where was he?

He started checking through the simple stuff. He was in his room onboard the Eos. He was certain about that as he recognised his clothes from where he had thrown them the night before. But it was quiet, too quiet. The engines were silent. There was no continuous throb of power throughout the very fabric of the ship.

Was he still dreaming?

Had the gaggle of girls taken over the ship?

Or had they landed on Triassica?

Having learnt his lesson from the previous day he stopped only long enough to pull on some clean clothes and brush his teeth before scrambling towards the galley. Inside he found only Nattie and Fuzz ball having breakfast.

"Where are…?" started Torr

"…our passengers? They left early this morning. They wanted to get to the Theme Park. Apparently there's a new Circus attraction they urgently want to see," finished Nattie, wiping her lips daintily with a napkin.

"The Circus? Isn't that a bad idea?" Torr asked, every atom of his being urging caution.

"I thought you'd be pleased. I know they were annoying you…"

"Nattie! The Circus!"

Their eyes met in alarm.

"Not…"

"Dr…"

"Wunderfoul's..."

"Weird and Wonderful..."

"...Circus?"

"It couldn't..."

"...be?"

Kiki's cheerful voice entered the conversation, "Do you want to go to the circus? I can find every circus within a day's travel. Just say the word!"

Torr and Nattie both studiously ignored him as their eyes remained locked together in a final moment of hesitation before there was an explosion of action. Chairs fell to the floor, arms and legs flew in different directions and handfuls of food were thrust into open mouths.

They'd met Dr Wunderfoul when pursuing the Second Celestial Secret. He was insanely dangerous and they'd only just escaped with their lives. He'd threatened to get even. The girls might not be as lucky as they had. Additionally, they didn't know what they were facing and they had no Kezin to get them out of trouble.

Nattie was the first to speak, "You get the bag, I'll pack!"

"I just hope that we get to them on time. Kiki, you'd better come with us."

"Fuzz ball?" called Nattie.

Fuzz ball looked up from where she was spreading another layer of thick chocolate sauce onto a chocolate donut apparently unfazed by the flurry of activity. The mound of chocolate twirled upwards with dainty precision; an artificial architecture of candied confusion.

"...You too!"

Fuzz ball stared at Nattie for one long moment and then swallowed the chocolate covered donut in a single mouthful before emptying her glass of chocolate flavoured milk with a solitary gulp. There was a momentary hilarious vision of chocolottarama before she licked the chocolate moustache from her lips and started to squeeze herself out of her chair. There was a very good reason why she was called Fuzz **ball** and it wasn't because she had a healthy lifestyle.

~o0o~

The main theme park on Triassica was Saurox and it wasn't hard for Torr and his friends to find. At the entrance there were a pair of giant tusks creating a huge arch, followed immediately by the tumultuous rib cage of some giant dinosaur that framed a macabre tunnel through which all guests were ushered.

Without warning, Fuzz ball suddenly leapt into Nattie's arms as a whiplash crack lashed the air beside them.

"I'll show you lazy lizard man!" screamed an enraged and evil looking human with a long, silver, metallic whip in his hand. He was threatening a young lizard boy who had stumbled with a tray of drinks.

"Clear up this mess and get back to work!" he screamed as he beat at the boy with his fists.

Nattie gripped Torr's arm fiercely, "That's terrible. Someone should do something about it," she whispered.

"I know. It goes on everywhere, though, not just in the circus. People are persecuted for what they look like rather than who they are and what they do. Some people just look like monsters, whilst others act like them."

"Why aren't there Celestial Secrets that stop people being horrible to each other?"

Torr thought for a moment but no answer was forthcoming and then he remembered something that he'd heard a long, long time ago.

"For there to be good there must also be evil so that we have something to compare it against. Without evil, what is good?"

It didn't sound like the sort of thing that his Uncle Otto would have said. Was it some long lost memory of his father? He didn't know and at the rate they were going he was never going to find out. Reuniting with his parents always seemed to take second place to some more pressing emergency. It was beginning to really annoy him.

Whilst he wanted to help the lizard boy he was already on a mission. Several missions in fact and all of them were stopping him looking for his parents. He started to count them off on his fingers. Right now he was trying to make sure that some passengers he hardly knew were safe, then he had four more Celestial Secrets to recover, two evil empires to defeat. Only after all of those could he then start trying to find his parents who, as far as he knew, were lost near a black hole which he had no idea of the location of.

How could they have allowed this to happen? Didn't they care about how he'd feel?

All of this on what was an almost empty stomach. Some days he wished he were someone else. Well, almost anyone else, he corrected himself and certainly not the lizard boy. Suitably chastened by the realisation that there was always someone worse off than you he quit prevaricating and together they hurried on.

The entrance to the Circus was just inside the theme park and the big posters displayed interlocking scenes of fun and daring do. There was no sign, nor hint of Dr Wunderfoul and Nattie relaxed her grip on Torr's arm.

"You never know we might get a chance to have some fun ourselves," she laughed while pins and needles crawled over Torr's fingers as feeling reluctantly returned.

Torr joined her as he thought about how long it had been since they had both had a good time without looking over their shoulders, worried about who might be creeping up on them.

"Yes, let's go and relax for a change," he agreed, desperately trying to make it true.

~oOo~

The circus was indeed fun and by the end of the first half, all of them were enjoying themselves so much that their sides ached from an over abundance of mirth. There was no denying that there was a dark undertone to some of the acts but the group laughter and amusement of the crowd was difficult to resist.

Torr felt that he shouldn't find the antics of the lizard clowns funny. But he couldn't help himself when they were wearing their clown suits and being chased around the arena by a pack of hungry lions. The funniest moment was when one of the lions had caught a lizard man by his tail and everyone thought he was finished. The unfortunate clown was thrown into the air and as he somersaulted upwards he somehow shrugged free of his tail as if it wasn't real.

Back down on the ground the lion looked puzzled and perplexed at the sudden escape. Lizards shouldn't do that. Lions couldn't.

The crowd just roared with laughter and clandestine hilarity. Torr had heard that lizards could she their tails but he'd never actually seen it before.

Nattie kept looking around, wondering if she would be able to see their temporary passengers anywhere but there was no sign of them. Technically they were no longer her passengers and therefore not her concern. But that didn't stop her being anxious about them. Her stomach rumbled in agitated sympathy.

"I'm feeling hungry, I didn't get a chance to finish breakfast," she announced.

She glanced around, "Look, there's a hot dog seller."

Torr reluctantly tore his attention away from the circus ring and gazed over to the back of the tent towards where she was pointing. He could smell the hot dogs and his stomach growled in anticipation. His eyes met Nattie's and their stomachs sent silent messages of agreement.

"I'll get some!" she announced and shot off.

Torr concentrated back on the centre ring where preparations seemed to be underway for an escape artist and illusionist. He watched closely to see if he could spot how the trick was constructed but the stage was full of too many distractions.

There were large vats of boiling liquid, chains, flamethrowers, buzz saws, acid locks, smoke, mirrors, spiked balls, long swords and a singular, small, half drunk, glass of water. For some insane reason they all needed to be individually introduced by a scantily clad, exotically dressed, electric blue lizard woman. Something about the way she seemed to be looking straight at his seat captivated him and he found himself staring back at her, mesmerised.

The bright lights flashed and dazzled his eyes that unnaturally refused to blink. Did her blue skin mean she was possibly a distant relative of Zarrox, the Keeper of the Secrets? His eyes were firmly fixed forwards in frank felicitation and his mind drifted, he knew not where. He felt strangely sleepy but also drawn to watch with rapt attention. As far as his brain was concerned, watching this act was the singular most important thing in the universe.

But no matter how closely he watched her he couldn't see the secret behind the trick. His attention had been enticed too far into a labyrinthine snare of mental entrapment. Along with the rest of the crowd he gasped in amazement at the stunning finale before breaking into cheering applause that threatened to deafen him.

Another fascinating act followed and then another. It was only when his stomach renewed its complaints that he realised Nattie hadn't returned. There were no welcome hotdogs to quench his unsatisfied craving.

What was keeping her? How long did it take to buy a hotdog?

He looked around for her in all directions but neither Nattie, nor the hot dog vendor, were anywhere to be seen. Where could she be? Was she lost, or worse?

Torr's stomach sank and hid under the seat in shame. He'd let his guard down and let himself get distracted. Alarm bells started going off in his brain. Now he'd lost track of Nattie. If his earlier suspicions were correct…

…they couldn't be, could they?

Torr berated himself for not paying more attention to what Nattie was doing and where she was. But the performance had been so engrossing that he hadn't noticed the time passing.

The lights started to flash again to announce the next performer and Torr found himself becoming engrossed again in the preparations for what he was sure would be another remarkable act.

His stomach growled at him, louder this time, half in hunger and half in contemptuous disgust that his brain could be so easily distracted. He shook his head to try and clear it, once... twice...

Think, he had to think. Why was he finding it so hard to think?

What was important here?

Hot dogs!

He shook his head again. Not hot dogs, but something to do with hot dogs.

Nattie! That was it, Nattie.

The lights flashed more urgently and Torr felt his concentration slipping once more. Anxiously he clung to that one thought of Nattie whilst his consciousness wrestled to resist the allure of the circus.

"Nattie, Nattie, Nattie, hot dogs, Nattie", he found himself saying out loud.

With sudden realisation his brain fitted the pieces of the puzzle together and he recognised what was going on. Something, no, more probably someone, was trying to stop him thinking about Nattie.

Harnessing his determination and willpower, Torr focused resolutely on Nattie. The hypnotic illusion of the circus illuminations shattered like an ornate picture window and he found himself staring at the obvious conclusion with clear certainty. Why would anyone want to stop him thinking about Nattie, unless they had sinister motives?

To Torr, if Nattie hadn't returned for sinister reasons, that could mean only one thing.

Chapter 4: Kidnapped!

In a panic, Torr leapt from his seat and raced up the steps towards the back of the huge circus tent without looking back. He didn't want to take any chances. He'd been mesmerised once, he wasn't going to let it happen again if he could at all avoid it.

Horrible images flashed through his mind about what might be happening to Nattie. Besides, what chance would he have to find the rest of the Celestial Secrets without her? He didn't even want to think about the possibility. If anything had happened to her…

Kiki buzzed up alongside of him and interrupted Torr's dire line of thought.

"Torr… Where are you going?"

"Nattie's…"

"What is it?"

"…been kidnapped!"

"Where are you going?"

"I'm sure of it."

"But…"

"But nothing."

"…what about…"

"Nattie's the most important thing here," Torr raged.

"But, but, but the..." Kiki insisted.

"Less arguing, more running! Now shut up and help me find her!" Torr shouted.

Fuzz ball momentarily looked away from the show and realised she was now sitting alone. Immediately, she glanced around and seeing Torr disappearing behind her she leapt to her furry feet and hurried after him, already heavily panting in lukewarm pursuit.

Within moments, Torr had reached the crest of the seating, with Fuzz ball gasping along far behind him. Looking directly below the top of the seating, down towards the bottom of the exit staircase he glimpsed a lizard man disappearing from sight into a canvas tunnel. He appeared to be carrying something pink.

Could that be Nattie?

Nattie had been wearing a pink top.

Torr ran faster.

"Kiki, catch me!" called Torr and without further thought leapt from the top railing towards the ground far below.

This was the quickest way to get down to where the lizard man had already disappeared into the gloom of the under seating area. Torr just hoped Kiki wasn't going to choose this particular moment to go into an unhelpful sulk for more than a millisecond.

"What...?" squawked the totally surprised electronic contraption and wheeled after the falling figure at full throttle.

Torr dropped from the high railing like a stone, trailing his hands high above his head. He silently prayed that this was going to work. He hadn't had time to brief Kiki on what he was planning.

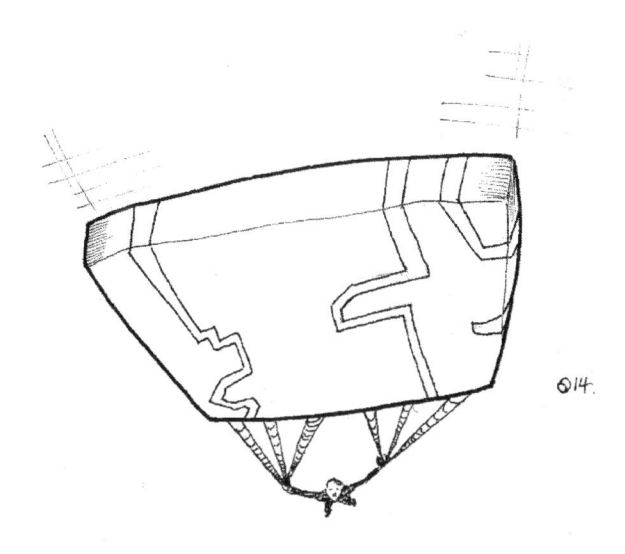

With a burst of much needed speed Kiki grabbed him by the wrists and deployed a large parachute canopy moments before Torr's legs turned into a shattered gooey mess of splintered bones. The two of them skidded and sprawled across the sawdust-strewn sand.

"Next time…"

"You had me going there…"

"…give me some more warning… my predictive circuits can be a little temperamental."

"…thought you weren't going to make it," wheezed Torr Fuzz ball stared down at them from the balcony far above.

"Don't jump!" Torr whispered loudly, hoping that she could hear him. He wasn't sure whether Kiki could repeat the same trick with someone of Fuzz ball's mass.

The cute ball of fur and hugginess started down the steps. Almost immediately she stumbled, ending up bouncing her way into a crumpled furry heap at the bottom before getting caught up in the fabric of the parachute. She dragged herself up contemptuously, wiped the sawdust off of her furry nose whilst giving Torr a withering look. He replied with a shrug that left her with no option but to kick his ankle, hard.

"Ow!" Torr yelped. "Look, I'm sorry you fell down the stairs, okay. But can we please get on with rescuing Nattie? I'm sure she's been kidnapped and I think I saw someone carrying her away in this direction."

Fuzz ball looked remorseful.

"I know, I know," he said, soothingly stroking the top of her head. "I feel the same. Let's just hope she's okay and I'm just imagining the whole thing."

Despite his attempts to convince Fuzz ball that there was nothing to panic about, Torr was convinced there was.

He took in his surroundings. The canvas tunnel lay ahead of them, gloomy and filled with foreboding. Silhouetted against the light from the far end was the figure of the lizard man still shouldering his burden. His strange walk swayed erratically from side to side and his long tail swept the sawdust floor into clouds of dust behind him.

Surely, thought Torr, it had to be Nattie that he was carrying. Didn't it?

Fuzz ball's fur bristled as she prepared to chase after them at full speed.

Torr laid a restraining hand on her shoulder. This needed thinking and planning but Nattie was the one who normally did all of that. He tried to think like she thought. It hurt and he wasn't very good at it. Instead his mind overflowed with questions.

Where was the lizard man taking her?

Why was he taking her?

Why wasn't she struggling?

Was she dead?

Unfortunately, his brain was only focusing on questions that had nasty, cold, hard answers. Torr didn't actually think she was dead. Although he had to admit, it was more of a case of hopeful guesswork than any sort of informed opinion.

Thinking wasn't as easy as Nattie made it look, thought Torr. The baser instincts in his brain just wanted to agree with Fuzz ball. It kept insisting all of these questions weren't getting them anywhere and the more important thing was to get on with rescuing Nattie. At the moment he had no idea how he was going to do that but he wasn't going to let that stop him from doing something, anything.

It looked like Fuzz ball had been right in the first place. Torr turned and started to race down the canvas tunnel and a moment later Fuzz ball puffed along behind.

"Torr, wait!" Kiki called after the fleeing figures.

Although they were running too hard to hear Kiki's words, Torr still skidded to a halt at the end of the canvas tunnel. A moment later Fuzz ball cannon-balled into his legs nearly catapulting him straight out of the shadows. Somehow he stood his ground.

In front of them, the entrance opened out into a wide arena where they would be noticed as soon as they left the shelter of their hiding place. Torr's sense of self-preservation had cut in at just the right moment. Now was a time for sneakiness and subterfuge.

Looking all around him, Torr noticed that gaudily decorated trailers encircled the edges of the arena. Overhead, a second enormous canvas tent obscured what passed for sky inside of an asteroid. Whilst Torr didn't think the tented space was as immense as the big top, he couldn't be sure. At ground level, the centre was occupied by a small group of lizard men who appeared to be eagerly expecting the new arrival who Torr had been pursuing. He was still carrying the mysterious pink burden.

If it was Nattie, what did the lizard men want with her, he asked himself again. But he still had no answers.

He edged back into the cover of the tunnel again. Even though it was a small group of lizard men there were more than enough of them to prevent him from barging his way into the centre of the circle and demanding the return of his friend. They would easily overpower him, besides he'd look really stupid if it wasn't Nattie and the bundle was just a pile of pink sheets.

But he couldn't shake the feeling that there was something going on here. He needed to stay cautious though, he still didn't know enough about this asteroid and what the local laws were to allow him to act with abandon. Each of the asteroids had their own local customs. Maybe the lizard men had local rights over girls dressed in pink. Maybe it was a local carnival or tribal festival, who was he to judge others?

Only those asteroids controlled by Empires had any consistency in their laws and Triassica wasn't one of them. He needed to tread carefully. He was painfully aware that he still needed a plan, which at the moment was number one on a long list of things he was missing. He also couldn't get over a growing, worrying feeling that he'd forgotten something, or someone. But who?

There was a burst of laughter and the group of lizard men dispersed. The one who had been carrying the pink bundle heaved it back over his shoulder before carrying it into one or the trailers.

A sudden, deep, melodious bellow echoed across the sky like a distant thunderclap. But this wasn't a natural noise and as the strange sound trailed off it into a cry that was almost plaintive it abruptly ended with a snarling growl that left no room for misinterpretation. Whatever it was came from the nasty side of the street. Torr's skin cringed and wanted to hide.

"What was that?"

"If I'm not mistaken that was Draco Magnificat Necrom," whispered Kiki in one of his best matter of fact voices from his hiding place behind one of Torr's ears.

Torr hadn't heard Kiki catch them up, but that wasn't unusual.

"What?"

"That's a black dragon to you and me!"

"What's a Draco Magni-Cat Neck Long doing here? I thought dragons were just the stuff that myths and legends were made from."

Kiki leapt into full teacher mode, "What you have to realise, Torr, is that there are an awful lot of asteroids and that provides immense scope and opportunity for diverse development. Where do you think all of the lizard men and lion boys come from? They're genetic offshoots that are a direct by product of uncontrolled tampering with human genes. Well, in the case of dragons I suspect lizard and avian genealogy but I'm sure even your limited intelligence can catch my drift. They have a lot in common. What we consider to be 'modern', or 'natural' birds and lizards are both directly descended from the dinosaurs and this theme park proves the possibilities inherent in controlled genetic manipulation. I'm afraid though that research into the creation of mythical creatures is frowned upon in polite society..."

Torr looked surprised about what he was only half listening to.

"...and if genes are being tampered with in an uncontrolled fashion then there's no telling what other genetic engineering might also be going on. Dragons are only one of the possibilities."

Moments passed while Kiki left a pregnant pause that Torr had missed his intro for.

"What do we do now?" Torr finally asked after the wispy thread of conversation had withered and expired.

Kiki remained strangely silent. He'd expected just a little wonder and awe from his announcements about what might be taking place in secretive genetic laboratories across the solar system. Torr's disinterested ignorance verged on the insulting and only added to the wounded feeling that had been tickling his circuits since he'd been ignored back in the big tent.

"Come on Kiki," Torr prompted him. "You're always full of ideas when I don't need them. How about coming up with some clever rescue plan for Nattie?"

"Hmmph!" sniffed the electronic contraption. "We don't know yet that it is Nattie."

His child friendly circuits were making it tough for him to deliberately remain difficult, however.

"You might want to try the overnight bag. That usually has something useful inside," he suggested.

"The overnight bag? Where is it?" grumbled Torr as he searched the floor around him. Where had he left it?

"Well, let me see..." said Kiki in a sarcastic tone. "Would that be the overnight bag I was trying to remind you about when you insisted on running from the main arena before jumping to your death? The one that you carelessly left behind you?"

"Yes, that would be the one!" grumbled Torr, kicking at the sawdust in frustration. "Come on, we'd better go and get it and hope that nothing happens to Nattie whilst we're gone."

"That won't be necessary," replied Kiki.

There was a scrambling sound high above them and then the overnight bag sailed through the air before landing in a crumpled heap and a muted thud at the other end of the tunnel they had just come from. Running full pelt down the canvas corridor it jumped into Torr's arms as if it was a long lost puppy.

There was a faint sound of impact bags deflating as it landed in his arms, or was it just a grateful sigh?

"How...?" queried Torr. "Never mind, it's here now."

He began rummaging inside the bag to see whether there was anything that might resemble the beginning of a plan.

"There's nothing inside except for this," he announced pulling a small cap with a rather large letter 'H' on the front, from the bag. It looked like it was his size, but based on his previous experience he decided it was probably a good idea to inspect it carefully before trying it on for size.

Running his hands over the fabric, it felt crisp to the touch. Peeling back the interior lining he saw a fine weave of wires and electronic components. The whole fabric of the hat was interlaced with sophisticated, delicate, electronics.

"It certainly looks like nothing I've ever seen. Is it of alien origin?"

"If my mythology data banks are up to date then it's probably the Hyper Automated Denial of Electronic Surveillance Cap, or as otherwise known, the HADES cap," Kiki said in his usual annoying, patronising tone, neatly side stepping Torr's last question.

"It doesn't look old enough to be mythological. It looks to be technological. What does it do?"

"Based on a cursory understanding of the circuitry, I'd say it was designed to make the wearer invisible. It should work."

"I really don't like that word 'should'," murmured Torr. "How will I know if it's working. I'm going to look pretty stupid wandering around thinking I'm invisible when I'm not. Isn't that a bit like the Emperor with no clothes?"

"Beats me," replied Kiki. "That piece of information hasn't been given to me yet. But if you find out then let me know and I can tell the next wearer."

Torr sighed loudly, "Yeah… the next wearer of course. Give them my regards." He bent down to his furry companion. "Fuzz ball, you'd better stay here. You're hardly less invisible."

Moments later, Torr was cautiously making his way towards the trailer that the pink bundle had been carried into. The cap appeared to be working as the lizard men appeared not to see him but you could never be too certain, especially with items from the overnight bag. It might stop working at any moment. Gently he made his way up the wooden stairs, grateful that the ancient planks didn't creak and opened the door.

He immediately regretted it. He might be invisible, but the door wasn't! As soon as he opened it, a startled lizard man who was seated inside looked up in shock and astonishment.

"Who'sssss there?" he hissed, staring straight through where Torr was standing in the entrance.

Torr scolded himself for being so stupid. What could he do now?

Chapter 5: Guess who?

Torr froze as the lizard man looked directly at him, readying himself for the imminent shout of alarm and subsequent attack. But it never came.

Instead, the lizard man's gaze never faltered as he got out of his seat, walked straight towards the doorway and grabbed the handle, pulling it wide to see if there was anyone hiding behind it. Desperate to avoid the lizard man bumping into him, Torr squeezed himself carefully past to avoid being shut in the entranceway. Seeing nothing, the lizard man pulled the door closed with a noisy creak of rusting hinges.

"Mussst be a faultssy catch," the lizard man muttered as he passed Torr, close enough to touch and returned to a small group of lizard men, clustered at one end of the caravan.

Apart from the lizard man who had got up to close the door they didn't appear to have any inclining that Torr might be in the carriage. Their attention was totally focused on the images displayed on multiple screens that flickered continuously, casting cold shadows throughout the remaining interior of the circus caravan.

Now that he was inside, Torr could see that there were interconnecting walkways between each coach, transforming the interior into a long, slim, room. There was only light at the end where he had entered. The other appeared to be dominated by a collection of large animal cages. From where he stood he couldn't tell what unnameable creatures might be in those captive heaps, secreted in the darkness.

For a moment, Torr considered getting closer to the lizard men to establish what they were watching, but that was risky. If he should accidentally bump into one of them he might be discovered. He decided he had more important things to worry about than what they were watching. The pink bundle had to be here somewhere, he'd seen it brought in. If he could just find it he could finally establish whether it was Nattie. He was sure it must be in amongst the cages and he resolved to investigate the sad, pathetic contents more closely.

There was a flash of pink amongst what appeared to be a pile of sleeping bodies in the nearest cage. At least he hoped they were sleeping. Torr held his breath and looked closer. Three of the bodies belonged to the triplets they had given a lift to following the incident with the Santa Anna the previous day, (there couldn't be three other identical girls in the same asteroid) and as he suspected the fourth was Nattie.

Well at least he had found her without a whole lot of searching and she was relatively safe for the moment, although what the lizard men wanted her for wasn't clear. Torr strongly suspected that 'relative' was a suspicious word in these circumstances and he would need to keep a close eye on it. Now, what to do about rescuing Nattie?

Whilst Torr felt a modicum of responsibility for the triplets, Nattie was his prime concern. If he could help them while rescuing Nattie he would, but rescuing her had to come first.

He took a closer look at the screens that had the full attention of the lizard men at other end of the long room. Screens flashed news feeds from across the asteroid chain and observation cameras secreted around the occupied areas of Triassica. A large number of the screens were focussed on the crowds in the circus arena. That explained how they had been spotted, but why were Nattie and the triplets important to them?

As he edged closer, he realised that the lizard men weren't actually paying any attention to the vast majority of the screens. They were only concentrating on a single channel. It must be important, but from where he was standing he couldn't see what they were watching.

Despite his concerns about being discovered Torr felt compelled to find out and he edged forwards cautiously. Trying to move invisibly without bumping into anyone was easier in thought than action. He had to carefully edge and thread his way into the crowd and strain his neck to see past the close knit throng of lizard men clustered around a single screen.

Finally he could see what they could see. It wasn't a news feed or entertainment channel; it was a single man speaking directly to the gang of lizard men in the caravan. But Torr couldn't listen to what was being said. As soon as he'd seen the face at the other end a stab of fear pinned his personality down and froze his blood solid in his veins. It was a face he would never forget. It was the face of Dr Wunderfoul.

If Kiki had been right that Kezin the lion boy was the result of some gene splicing experiment then it really was no surprise to find that Dr Wunderfoul was also involved in another circus full of mad, cross breeding, gene splicing, trans-cloning, animal experiments.

~oOo~

Aboard the Dragon's Storm, Lady Medea stormed off the bridge in a flounce of feathers, leaving her first mate to bring her ship into land at the space port inside Triassica. She was still fuming at those interfering children. Curse them! If it hadn't had been for the children she would already be heading for the Deep Redark of Heartness with a cargo-hold full of valuable, highly ransomable, child hostages.

Annoyed, she scratched at where the metalloid armour she was wearing rubbed her delicate skin. The constant irritation made her all the more irate and pushed her temper to flash point.

Well, revenge was a dish best served cold and she was personally going to reserve a frozen piece of hard dirt to bury those interfering brats in. No one crossed Lady Medea and lived!

With the help of the tracking device she'd planted on their space suits she knew exactly where they were. She would always know where they or at least their space suits were. She could wait and pick her moment, when they were least expecting it. It would just be a matter of time before they were in her hands and then... and then...

At the moment her mind was blank and didn't have the details. But she'd think of something interesting to fill it with. Something so horrific and terrifying that they'd never cross anyone again. Ever!

~oOo~

Torr tried to unpin his fascinated attention. He was looking straight into the viewing screen and it looked like Dr Wunderfoul was looking directly back at him. That couldn't really be happening, he was invisible. Wasn't he? Surely, the evil madman couldn't see him. Could he?

With large helpings of caution, he tried to keep a lid on his fear, rising panic and all round sense of loathing that stuck in his throat at the sight of the baneful, monstrous, Doctor. He forced himself to listen carefully.

"Well done, my minions," Dr Wunderfoul was saying. "Which of you was it that overheard the three girls talking about that despicable Torr Naydo and his companions?"

Torr's hairs prickled at the mention of his name. There was no doubt that the evil madman hadn't forgotten all about him.

One of the lizard men raised his hand. Torr noticed absently that the back of it was hard and scaly. There was a small section of skin between each of the fingers. Or were those claws? Torr was never sure on the correct nomenclature for genetically bred monstrosities. You always had to be so careful about offending them.

Torr corrected himself. Lizard men in themselves weren't evil just because they were lizard men. There were probably some very civil and polite lizard men somewhere. But these lizard men were in cahoots with Dr Wunderfoul and that meant there really wasn't much chance that they were going to get any awards for gallantry or 'lizard man of the year'.

Dr Wunderfoul was speaking again and Torr's ears clicked to attention.

"I knew that if I kept looking I'd get my revenge eventually. The solar system just isn't immense enough to hide them from my wrath. How did you discover them? What was it that gave them away?"

The lizard man hissed in reply, "It was the 'thhhree 'irlsss. 'thhhey 'ave him away when 'thhey were talking about how heroic and handsssome he looked."

Torr's brow furrowed, handsome and heroic? Him? He was the least heroic person he knew. Yuck! Girls were weird.

But he needed to keep listening in case he missed anything. Dr Wunderfoul was talking again.

"...triplets are particularly interesting as well. They remind me of some interesting research on group minds I read about recently. Maybe I even wrote it... I must remember to look up what it was. Now, tell me more about what you discovered, tell me everything. No piece of information is too small, or unworthy, to be fitted into the giant puzzle that mankind calls the Universe."

The lizard man reluctantly started to speak again.

"We knew it had to be the same Torr when they talked about how he had his own ssspace ssship. It was then that we desssided to sssee if we could find him. We found the girl. If hisss female mate isss here as well then he mussst be clossse by. We have teamsss out sssearching the asssssteroid for him now."

Female mate, thought Torr. What were they talking about? If they meant what he thought they meant then lizard men must be even more stupid than he'd first thought.

"Yes, he will certainly try and rescue her," Dr Wunderfoul was saying. "You must be vigilant and capture him. If you do, there will be a reward. Now get out there and find him, because if you don't then all of you will wish you'd never been hatched! Each and every one of you!"

Dr Wunderfoul jabbed his finger at the screen and ended the transmission. The lizard men glared around at each other, shrugging, hissing and spitting in a language that Torr couldn't quite grasp. He pressed himself up against the wall of the caravan as they bustled towards the exit leaving him alone in a deserted caravan with four sleeping girls.

Could it really be this simple, he thought, seeing a bunch of keys hanging up on the wall by the door to the cage. Surely they wouldn't fit, or there'd be some alarm that he hadn't deactivated. But he couldn't see one and the first key he tried appeared to turn in the lock quite smoothly.

Maybe his luck was changing?

Warily he opened the door to the cage and it was then that the next dilemma arose. If anyone entered the caravan whilst he was inside with the girls they'd re-lock the door. That was an easy one to fix, he thought as he slipped the keys into his pocket. Now no one could lock him in.

He shook Nattie awake first and then together they woke the triplets.

"Who is that? Torr, is that you? Why can't I see you?" Nattie muttered sleepily, rubbing at the back of her head.

He'd forgotten that he still had the Hades cap on. Smoothly he removed it and shoved it into his back pocket.

She gasped.

"Oh gosh, that cap is so clever. Where did you get it? No, don't tell me, let me guess. Was it the overnight bag?" she cooed, by which time the triplets were beginning to awake.

"Cool. Have you..."

"... got one, for..."

"... each of us?" the triplets asked and they all stared adoringly at him in a way that made Torr feel extremely uncomfortable. He wasn't used to being watched so closely.

His stomach felt weak. The hissing words of the lizard men echoed hauntingly in his ears; heroic and handsssome. The three identical faces staring hopefully at him gave him an unpleasant feeling and he tried to look away, which was difficult in the close confines of the caravan.

But his dilemma wasn't about to release him so easily and slapped him with every syllable of the triplets' disjointed sentence. Here they were with just one Hades cap between the five of them, trapped in a caravan, surrounded by lizard men and one, or more black dragons. How were they going to escape without being seen and what did Dr Wunderfoul have to do with it all?

Chapter 6: Dragon!

Torr stared in horror at Nattie.

Nattie stared in dismay at Kara.

Kara stared at Sara with no expression on her face.

Sara stared at Tara and Tara stared at her feet.

Not one of them had a single idea between them.

Destiny nudged fate who'd fallen asleep in a corner. He awoke with a grunt and rolled over. He thought about snoring.

Suddenly with a rip and a tear, accompanied with a grumbling roar, the roof of the huge tent was torn asunder as a black dragon descended towards the sawdust, ably assisted by a heavy dose of gravity. The confined space gave the dragon limited room to use his wings to control his fall, so he didn't so much land as hit and bounce. At least that was what he probably said to the other dragons when they all laughed about it later.

THE FOURTH SECRET
email: astro.saga.oblique.media@gmail.com

Inside the confined spaces of the caravans each

tumbling concussion created a wall of sound that battered their ears into submission. Outside, clouds of sawdust lifted into the air, creating an annoying,

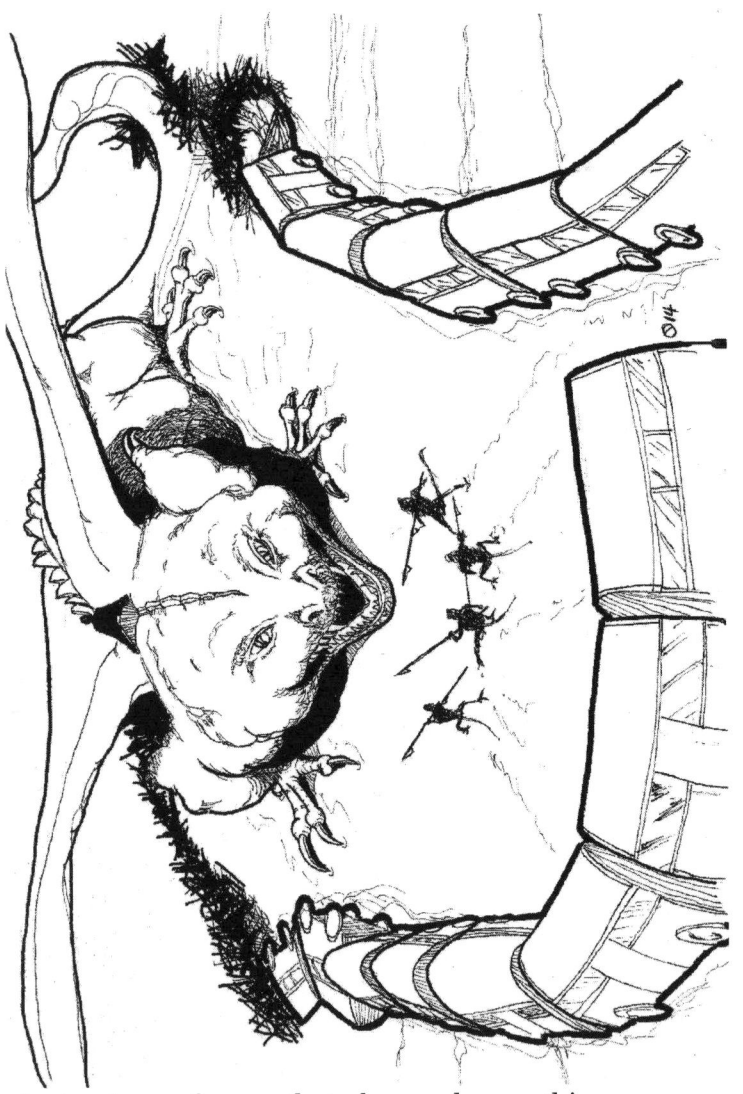

cloying haze of smog that obscured everything.

As introductions go, it was quite an entrance.

Despite the shaky and somewhat undignified landing, the rider immediately called out in a loud, clear voice, "In the name of Lord Steal, I demand that you hand your captives over to the forces of the Aztex Empire!"

After the initial shock of the descending dragon the lizard men rallied well, picked themselves off of the ground and looked in the mood for an argument. Insanely, armed only with wooden weapons they confronted the dragon who contemptuously glared back at them. The stage was set for a fight and all it would take was one spark for the whole thing to ignite. And with dragons around the one thing you could be sure of was…

Torr looked at Nattie with a glint in his eye.

"Now?"

"Now?!"

"Now!?"

"Now!"

"Ummmm!" interrupted Kara.

"What do you…

"…mean, 'Um'?" finished Sara.

"Look…" started Tara.

"...out of the window!" screeched a sister.

No one stopped to identify which of the triplets had finished the sentence. Instead, they all tried dashing for the window at once. In the crush Torr realised that there was a situation worse than being shoved out of the way by Fuzz ball and that involved four teenage girls all fighting for viewing space at once. The wall of knees, elbows, hair and the residual clouds of sawdust totally obscured his view. He found himself at the back of the crowd with only Tara and Nattie having any chance of making sense of what was going on outside.

He slunk back from the overcrowded window and tried to think above all of the giggling and shrieking. Something felt very wrong but he just couldn't put his finger on what it was. Was it something to do with Fuzz ball, Kiki and the overnight bag outside amidst the bedlam of chaos? Were they staging some imaginative rescue plan?

Common sense came to his rescue and he concluded that the chances of that happening were as likely as the ground suddenly opening up and swallowing all of his problems for him. As if...

At the window the girls were trying to get his attention and tell him what was happening.

"The lizard men…" started Tara.

"…have teamed up with the rider …" added Sara.

"…of the dragon. They've…" finished Kara.

"…come to some form of …" continued Tara.

""…agreement and it appears …"

"…to involve us. Look, they're…"

"… heading this way. This should be fun," concluded Tara in a rush.

'What?' thought Torr. 'A moment ago there was going to be a fight and now… Now there was still going to be a fight and as usual he was going to be on the wrong end of it, again!'

Instinctively, they all backed away from the windows as the lizard men advanced towards them. Torr looked around for Nattie and his eyes caught her attention, Aghast, they locked on one another and Torr echoed the silent word she whispered with her lips, fun? What kind of word was that to use to describe what was going to happen next?

~oOo~

Far away, deep in the interior of the immense Saurox theme park in a cavern hidden at the end of a long valley, Tina fretted over her eggs. Whilst she had been genetically bred to grow to a size far beyond the scale of her ancestors, she still retained the basic instincts of all organisms large enough to observe without the aid of a microscope; racial survival.

The bloodline must survive.

The bloodline must grow.

The bloodline must thrive.

For some strange reason, to Tina's keen eye for detail, the nest no longer appeared to be big enough for all of the thriving that appeared to have been going on. Unfortunately, a tyrannosaurus rex's grasp of elementary arithmetic only went as far as 'I have one', 'I have none', 'I have many' and 'I'd like more'. So struggling with the concept of why 'many' had become 'many plus one' was as far beyond their comprehension as the finer elements of chaos theory were beyond the average butterfly.[1]

---

[1] Chaos theory proposes that some things are so complex that the outcome is impossible to predict from small variations in the starting point. Occasionally people try and explain this in terms of butterflies creating hurricanes, which is such an insanely difficult thing to believe that some people (and unbalanced computers) have gone as far as to state that chaotic theory is akin to chaotic thinking. A far easier example of chaos theory is the difficulty of throwing the same number twice in a row with a dice. No matter how hard you try to do exactly the same throw it invariably gives you a very different number and unless it gives you some advantage in the great game of life, why would you care anyway?

As a result, all Tina understood was that ever since she had foiled the attempt to steal one of her eggs something wasn't quite right. She might never win any prizes for mathematics, but no one could accuse her of being an untidy mother.

A cold wind blew an icy draft through the cave and she shivered. In a burst of very characteristic rage she banged the eggs together, forcing them to fit into the over stretched nest. A weakened crack collapsed under the stress and bleeding yoke, it broke inwards. The others heaved a sigh of relief as the pressure slackened and one, just one, slightly different from the rest, started humming softly to itself.

~o0o~

Before Torr and his loose collection of friends could share their emotional confusion verbally a giant rumble split the air. Everyone ducked and cowered for cover. Girls screamed. Pandemonium reigned and the grumbling rumble tumbled around the room, shocking the shrieking woodwork alarmingly. An intense light blinked instantaneously, flooding the shadows with incandescence. It hadn't originated inside the caravan. It had come from outside. Had the dragon launched its attack? Was a searing sphere of flame already on its way towards their caravan?

"What's going on!" Torr yelled above the terrifying noise.

"I don't know; it seems to be coming from beneath us!" screamed Nattie as shadows fled towards the ceiling from a menacing red glow that ominously made itself felt through the floorboards.

Light from beneath?

The air echoed the moaning ground as a huge bellow of thunder followed the white flash of another lightning bolt. The sky that could be seen through the rent tent was darkening by the second and the interior of the cabin had already descended into deepest gloom.

"Look, the ground's opening up!" shrieked Sara, who was still crouching by the window, peering cautiously out on the bedlam.

"…and the lizard…" wailed Kara from the floor.

"…men are falling in…" laughed Tara as she hid under a blanket.

The part of Torr's brain that was still thinking questioned why this was funny. What sort of person laughs in the face of certain death? Girls appeared to have no appreciation of how dangerous his life really was. No wonder he found it difficult to relate to them.

"...and the dragon's rider has gone too," continued Sara.

"...probably fell into the chasm..."

"...although the dragon's still there and coming this way," added Tara, her voice muffled by the blanket still over her head.

That's great, thought Torr. Just the way his luck went. Dangerous monster only kept in check by its trained rider. And who falls into the chasm to certain death? The rider of course, leaving a murderous beast to rampage unchecked!

ROBERT SMITHBURY
email: astro.saga.oblique.media@gmail.com

Chapter 7: Eruption

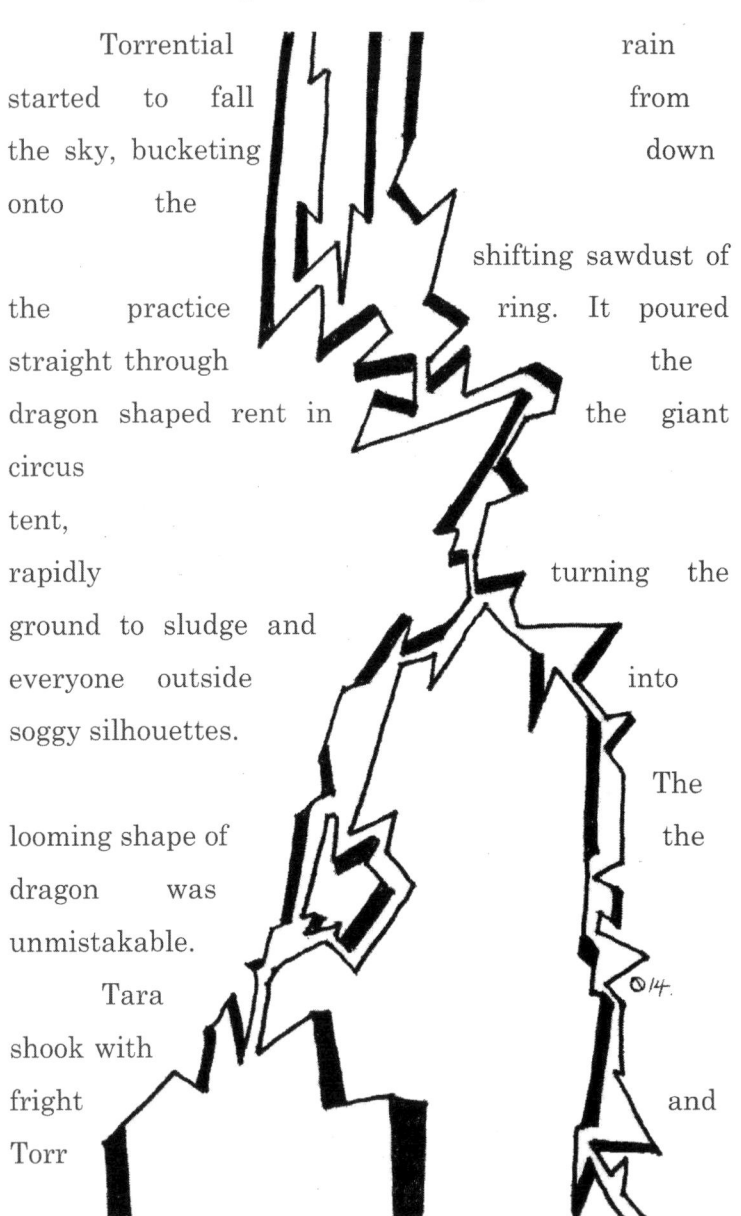

Torrential rain started to fall from the sky, bucketing down onto the shifting sawdust of the practice ring. It poured straight through the dragon shaped rent in the giant circus tent, rapidly turning the ground to sludge and everyone outside into soggy silhouettes.

The looming shape of the dragon was unmistakable.

Tara shook with fright and Torr

considered joining her under the blanket. Hang on a second, shouted the right side of Torr's brain to his left. If she's hiding beneath the blanket, how can she see anything from there? How could anyone know the dragon was still there from underneath a blanket? What was going on?

Torr knew he didn't have a very good understanding of girls in general, but the triplets were really beginning to freak him out. They were weird.

"All of the other lizard men are running away!" exclaimed Nattie. "Something has really frightened them this time."

Before Torr had a chance to connect this new idea to anything resembling relevance the caravan shifted precariously. They all slowly slid across the floor towards the only door.

The girls screamed helplessly as Torr tried to make sense of it all. Had the dragon grabbed the trailer? Were they dangling in the grip of certain death and imminent destruction, he wondered.

With the trailer door now facing the ground, gravity flipped it open, flailing wildly as the sodden sawdust floor beckoned just close enough to jump down to. But that would mean leaving the apparent safety of the caravan and facing the behemoth outside. Everyone clung to anything they could, fingers clawing at wooden boards for any sign of an indentation as they gradually continued to slide in a helpless pile towards the door. Rain fell like a waterfall. The floor of the arena, soaked to saturation point, started pooling into thick, oozing mud.

His fingers unable to grip any longer, Torr slid inexorably to the edge of the doorway.

That's wonderful, thought Torr, sarcastically. Just my luck that as I'm about to fall powerlessly from the caravan to the ground, it starts turning into a seething pool of mud and mire.

Having arrived first at the gaping exit to the caravan, Torr jammed himself against the sides of the wide-open doorway in an attempt to prevent a sludgy collision. The girls continued to slide towards him and bodies piled up, forcing him downwards as he struggled to maintain his grip on the creaking wooden doorframe.

There was another tremendous roar from just out of sight that held a promise of sharpened teeth and sulphurous breath. It sounded much closer than before and the flashes of lightening cast an ominous shadow across the ground towards them. If they'd known what it was they would have recognised the strong smell of brimstone that assaulted their senses.

With the weight of four girls on top of him Torr knew it was only a matter of moments before he would lose his hold on the door and they would all collapse to the soggy, muddy ground below. His grip was slipping.

The caravan lurched again and a crack in the ground opened up nearby. The split started to widen, threatening to engulf the slippery mud that beckoned beneath him. His whole world groaned. Being crushed by a mini mountain of girls in a caravan that was about to tip into a precipice, or dropping into a murky puddle ready to become dragon bait, didn't feel like much of a choice to Torr. The possibility that the asteroid itself might fracture, sucking them all out into the void of space, didn't help either.

Another sudden lurch of the ground took the choice away from him as his grip finally gave way under the flurry of female arms and legs. With a squawk of angry anticipation Torr collapsed onto the sodden ground. Around him the rain continued to lash down in icy pellets, soaking him instantly. Tara, Sara and Kara, landed atop him, knocking the breath out from his lungs whilst cold mud wormed its way into his ears.

The long, dark, inquisitive shadow of the dragon loomed large across them all. Some days it just wasn't worth getting dressed for. The crack zigzagged erratically closer towards them.

Nattie? Where was Nattie? Torr wondered as he fought to free himself from under the triplets. She didn't appear to be amongst them.

Nattie moaned from the doorway above him as the caravan lurched backwards after disgorging the first four children, sweeping her away towards the widening hole in the ground. She was rubbing her head with one hand while desperately holding on with another. Had she hit her head, Torr wondered.

Teetering near the edge of the crack in the ground, two of the caravan wheels slipped over the edge of the enlarged precipice and dangled in mid air, spinning idly. It didn't look very stable and any moment it threatened to tip over.

Nattie grunted. Her head hurt from where it had hit the door jam. Her eyes wanted to close. Torr? Where was Torr?

"Ooooh!" wailed Sara, sitting in a puddle.

"...This isn't fun..." continued Kara, splattered in mud.

"...We want our..." moaned Tara wiping slime from her eyebrows.

"...money back!" spluttered Sara.

Torr had almost succeeded in wriggling free. Looking up he could see the shaky, wooden undercarriage of the caravan as it hung dangerously over the enormous chasm that had opened up. A girl's arm dangled sadly from the open doorway. Instinctively he knew it had to be Nattie. No one knew how to get themselves stuck in a tricky situation better than Nattie. Granted she was usually the one who knew how to get them out of it again, but if she'd hit her head she wouldn't be thinking straight. Torr could tell she was in real trouble this time.

Another huge lightening bolt connected ground and sky as if to emphasise the need for instant action with an electric exclamation mark.

Torr launched himself through the air to grab hold of Nattie's arm as the caravan edged further to the edge.

Torr's sudden grip on her arm shocked Nattie back into the unwelcoming world of her predicament.

The caravan's wooden floorboards creaked and protested as they fought for stability amidst terrifying reality.

Torr? Why was Torr shouting at her?

"Nattie! Jump. The caravan's going over the edge," he yelled helplessly at her.

Too late, Nattie found herself slipping back across the floor.

With what sounded like a creaking cry of distress the caravan lost its struggle with gravity and the edge of the crevasse before slipping grumbling and grinding down the jagged sides into the darkness. With some degree of surprise but also relief, Torr found himself still holding Nattie's hand as she dangled over the precipice. Fortunately for both of them, the rest of Nattie was still comfortably attached to it, suspended over what was no doubt a very deep, dark drop into certain death.

But his muddy fingers were already beginning to lose their grip. Vainly he tried to hold on more tightly.

He dared a look downwards. With dismay he saw that oozing up from below, where Nattie's feet dangled a bubbling flow of lava was clawing its way up the fissure towards them. Nattie's weight hung heavily and he didn't have the strength to haul her in. Her eyes met his.

Time froze and Torr's brain disassociated itself from the impending peril. Questions clamoured for attention. Surely it wasn't normal for the ground to suddenly open up and for lava to come bubbling through or for thunderstorms to arrive, almost instantly from bright, blue skies? Clearly, the Fourth Secret had been disturbed somewhere and the resulting stress was making itself felt in the volcanic substructure of the asteroid. They were fortunate that the asteroid's crust appeared to be quite thick here.

The gentle slide of Nattie's wet fingers through his grip, assisted by the heavy rain and insidious mud dragged his mind back to the precarious reality of their predicament. He didn't have the strength to haul her up. If he didn't do something quickly, she was going to be consumed by the searing heat of the lava that was already snapping at the toes of her boots.

Chapter 8: From the frying pan...

Whilst Torr's mind whirled in confusion, a large black claw descended and encompassed both their hands. Its cold, scaly touch sent Torr's skin crawling and only the talon's iron grip prevented him from wrenching his hand free. There was a wild whimpering whine from somewhere nearby that had to be Nattie, thought Torr. At least she was still alive.

The dragon lifted them up until they both dangled helplessly in front of its awesome jaws. Torr gagged on the rotten stench of its breath. Pulsing, green venom dripped from its lips and glowing, hot coals stared at them from its eye sockets.

Typical, thought Torr, straight from the frying pan into the fire. He hadn't considered that their position could get any worse but it seemed that it just had.

There was a throaty grumble from the dragon and the sky rumbled an echoing response. The ground seemed to grunt and groan in unintended harmony. So these were sounds that heralded an impending doom, thought Torr and he tensed himself for an imminent toasting. About all he could hope for now was that their ending would be quick.

Lizard men started to cautiously re-enter the ripped and fragmented tent, picking their way carefully across the lava and rubble strewn floor as rain continued to pound down around them. The water hissed and spat as it made contact with the red hot, rising lava, creating fountains of steam that drifted in and out of the darkening shadows. It was difficult to make sense out of anything that could be seen.

Suddenly through the haze Torr thought he recognised one of the figures. It looked like Fuzz ball, no doubt with Kiki who would be too small to see at this distance, advancing carefully from the opposite direction to the lizard men. The overnight bag was unmistakably thrown across her shoulder.

Hope rose in his throat. Of course! The overnight bag would contain something useful although Torr reserved a tiny suspicion that it might only bring further frustration, too. Gingerly Fuzz ball slipped between overturned caravans and stepped across deep fissures carrying Torr's last vestige of futile expectation inexorably towards them.

Hurry, thought Torr silently as he continued to do his dangling impression of dragon bait.

Perhaps Kiki's lasers might... might... might what? It was no use, the bit of his brain that came up with good ideas couldn't think straight amidst the pandemonium. Instead it decided to conceal itself in a tiny hiding place it had spotted earlier. This was no time to be trying to attract attention to yourself.

In front of Torr the dragon's scaly lips parted and a small plume of smoke drifted out. Is this it, he thought. Am I about to become boy bacon burger for breakfast?

Nattie's whimpering was getting annoying as his ears filled with a high pitched crooning that made it even more difficult to think straight. Out of the corner of his eye he could see the triplets slithering around in the mud beneath them in a fit of giggles at his and Nattie's predicament. What on earth was funny? He couldn't see anything that was even slightly amusing.

They really did seem to be weird and incomprehensible.

The wailing reached a crescendo, threatening to deafen him before it softened into a soggy, sob. Wait a minute, wait a minute! That couldn't be Nattie whimpering, thought Torr. It was far too loud and the sound was coming from much closer. In fact, it was coming from right in front of his face.

It had to be the dragon that was whimpering! There was no other possibility. No matter how absurd it seemed, it had to be the enormous dragon with the eyeball from hell that was whimpering. It wasn't

Nattie at all. Why was something as big and ugly as a dragon crying?

Relief at the thought flooded through Torr.

"Nattie! Nattie, the dragon is crying!" Torr shouted unsympathetically.

"What?" Nattie groaned, still only half conscious and struggling to make sense of anything following the bump to her head.

Torr studied Nattie's face carefully. She was biting her lip and her face was wet and streaked, but that was probably the rain. He hoped it was just the rain.

"The dragon's crying. That's not normal is it?" he asked again, hopeful that she might be able to answer intelligently.

"No, it's not," answered Kiki's through his ear piece. "Hang on, Fuzz ball and I are almost with you. We need to get out of here quickly! I'm not quite sure how we are going to do that yet but hopefully by the time I get to you I'll have come up with something."

Kiki didn't sound very certain and Torr remained unconvinced.

Suddenly it occurred to Torr that the dragon was more afraid of the earthquake and storm than they were afraid of the dragon. The weather had certainly deteriorated sharply in the last few minutes. Without its rider the dragon had no one to guide and look after it. Maybe it was just a frightened at heart and needed someone to take charge. Maybe that someone could be Torr?

His instincts retook control.

"I think it's as scared as we are," shouted Torr above the sound of the thunderstorm. "I'm going to try and soothe it down and see if it will let me up onto it's back."

"Torr, don't!" wailed Nattie.

But it was too late.

Torr reached out his hand and scratched at the dragon's horny carapace. Close up he could see that the dragon wasn't black but a combination of deep, dark mauves, blues and browns. To his amazement the dragon scrunched up its face and crooned. It's grip on his other hand loosened for a moment. This seemed to be working.

Torr could see that time was running out and he didn't have long to make this work. The lizard men were closing in and he needed to act quickly. Taking a huge chance, he slipped his free hand around the dragon's neck and hauled himself up onto its back, dragging Nattie behind him as he did so. The dragon didn't seem to object as Torr fought to gain a safe position for them both amongst the rain soaked scales.

Finding a strap Torr slithered and followed it to the rider's seat. The dragon saddle consisted of a lot of leather, chains and even more harness straps that fed through a simple loop mechanism. Surprisingly there were multiple seats, with safety straps, weapons and pack bags slung in a wild variety of positions. This was a plus. Lots of room for everyone. This dragon was built for comfort. He started to dare to believe that things might be going his way.

New ideas were suddenly sneaking into Torr's mind faster than the rain slipped from his shoulders.

"Okay, all aboard! We're getting out of here," he shouted above the roar of the storm.

Chapter 9: Mush!

On the ground the triplets scampered to climb the dragon's sides as Kiki gave Fuzz ball an assisted lift to the top. Behind them the surrounding lizard men were now appearing feel a lot braver as they hurried across the ruined practice ring in hot pursuit.

Torr decided to investigate the weapons whilst he had a few free moments. There was a helmet and visor which when he tried it on, surprisingly, wasn't a bad fit. Nearby was a rather large sword, but Torr had already tried his hand at swordplay and wasn't about to waste energy hoping he could use it. As he'd expected there were no projectile or energy weapons but there was an interesting looking lance and a whip with sinister appearance. The handle of the lance had a number of controls built into the leather strapping but Torr didn't have the time to try and figure out what they did right now. Maybe later.

"Wow, a real…"

"…live dragon. This is…"

"… fantastic."

With some surprise Torr realised that he was getting used to the triplets habit of completing each other's sentences. It was still weird but given the rest of his life he was ready to live with it as a small inconvenience in the greater scheme of things. He still couldn't tell them apart, but if they were able to finish each other's thoughts off then he guessed it didn't really matter which one he was talking to, or who said what. Strangely, multiple mirror image siblings had their compensations.

Everyone was on board, just ahead of the lizard men and their relentless advance. He fed the reins through his fingers, feeling their texture and weight.

Kiki buzzed around Torr's head, "We're ready enough. Let's go."

Torr nodded, as long as he could get the dragon to agree, of course.

Scratching between its ears in a way that he hoped the creature found soothing Torr began to realise how little he knew about dragons. How did you get a dragon to 'go'? Disappointedly, he found that he had no idea. What had he been doing at school?

"Mush!!" he tried weakly, flicking the reigns.

There was no response.

The lizard men had now surrounded the dragon and were shouting up at them as the children dumbly sat astride the beast, waiting vainly for something to happen. One of the lizard men appeared to be in charge and was attempting to goad the others into some form of concerted action. The outlook wasn't good.

"Get them down from there!" he ordered, whilst jumping at the dragon's side in a vain attempt to grab any dangling leg.

Bit by bit the lizard men were overcoming their fear of the dragon. One of the crazier ones tugged at the dragon's muzzle but either he was beneath the dragon's attention or was just being ignored as it didn't appear to notice him. Encouraged by the dragon's inaction the lizard men became even more adventurous, shouting and jeering in their strange, hissing, voices.

Everyone on board the dragon was becoming more agitated. Nattie pulled at Torr's shoulder.

"Try again Torr!"

He was becoming desperate. Frantically, he jabbed his knees and heels into the dragon's neck and simultaneously hauled on the reigns. Ominously, the dragon slowly turned its face to look at Torr, making Torr feel as if its red baleful eye had just searched and examined the depths of his soul.

Torr suddenly felt very, very vulnerable. Then, with one eye still fixed firmly on Torr the dragon lifted its head and hauled the contemptuously brave lizard man into the air. The poor creature dangled helplessly trying not to scream and wishing it had never grabbed hold.

"Watch it!" the dragon growled.

At the sound of the dragon's voice Torr dropped the reigns in surprise and tried his best to look innocent.

"Who me?" he asked, hoping that the dragon would really be talking to the dangling lizard man.

"Yes, you. What are you pulling on the reigns for?"

"Err... I wanted you to get us out of here," Torr muttered guiltily with massive discomfort and embarrassment.

This wasn't going at all how he had expected.

"Well you just needed to ask politely. The reigns are just for show to make the idiot rider look like they're in charge. I'm a 20 tonne, black, flying dragon with firestorm breath that can incinerate a waterfall. A tiny bit of leather pulled by a barely evolved monkey isn't going to worry me a bit. I'm the one who's in charge here. Just you remember that. Now you treat me with the respect due of someone who could swat you like a gnat and tell me nicely where you want to go and then we might be at the beginning of getting somewhere."

Torr glanced around at the circle of lizard men. They had completely hemmed the dragon in on all sides, except one. There was no backing out now. He was in this for better, or worse. There was only one obvious direction to go.

"Um, up?"

"Are you sure about that?"

"Uh, I guess so."

"OK, I like up. Up it is!"

The dragon tensed its muscles and then leapt skywards. Everyone screamed and lizard men dropped away. Only the mad, crazy, possibly brave one managed to cling onto the dragon's muzzle and then instantly regretted not letting go much sooner. The dragon spread his huge wings and beat them with frantic fluidity as they erupted through the remnants of the tent's roof and skywards into the heart of the tempest.

The effects of the thunderstorm had been bad from inside the flapping tatters of the tent, but out here, rising fast into the darkening sky, the rain fell on them with the full force of a waterfall. Under the deluge, the last clinging lizard man glanced around him before reluctantly releasing his grip in a shriek of terror. Instantly, gravity took over and he plummeted to the distant ground, disappearing into the storm clouds far below. There was too much smoke, steam and driving rain to see how hard he hit the surface. With a sickening feeling and subsequent realisation of how high they had suddenly climbed Torr recalled his Uncle Otto's wise words on gravity. He had no inclination to test them out himself.

A wide arc of lightning crackled across the clouds, illuminating the sky around them. Torr scanned the sky nearby.

Black shapes dusted the clouds, their impossible bulk kept aloft by beating wings. All about them great beasts hung impossibly in the air. They were surrounded by a full flight of dragons!

The triplets cooed at the sight in mutual appreciation and Nattie fixed Torr with a withering look.

He looked back at her bleakly. What had he got them into now?

"Ooops?" he muttered meekly.

Chapter 12:
Riding the thunderstorm

Across the blasted sky, surrounded by deluge and the thick thunderclouds, lightning crackled. Above the din, Torr could hear the beating wings of the other dragons and occasionally make out their enormous flying forms as he wondered just how you kept a 20 tonne dragon aloft.

As his thoughts wandered, the other dragons maintained their distance.

"Quick, put this on," Nattie urged, pushing a long, extending cloak at Torr. "It'll be a good disguise and the rest of us can shelter underneath it."

In the midst of the storm, rain lashed at them and light barely warranted a mention. Nattie's face was hardly discernible, even in the momentary flashes of near-blinding brilliance from nearby lightening bolts. Torr could see enough to tell that rain streamed down her face as if she was standing in the shower. Torr couldn't remember the last time he'd ever seen weather this bad.

Fastening the heavy cloak around his neck Torr threw the hood across his head, masking his features. Behind him he felt the others crawl under the cloak's long train in a vain attempt to keep out of the relentless deluge. Almost magically, beneath him, the dragon heaved as it fought gravity with its huge, dark wings beating strongly. Clinging desperately to its shoulders he could feel the rhythmic throb of the giant's muscles beneath the cold scaly skin.

"Get in formation there!" roared a voice across the night, mixing with the last growls of the thunder's latest grumble.

Torr's head swivelled as he tried to figure out who the voice was talking to.

"Do you think he's talking to us?" asked Nattie's voice from behind him, still muffled by the cloak.

"He is talking to us," rumbled the dragon's voice from beneath them. "Flying in formation is very important. This is a dragon thing you monkeys wouldn't understand. It's crucial to be tidy about these things. Leave it to me, I know what I'm doing."

With a swooping motion the dragon dipped its left wing and wheeled in the direction that the voice had come from. Underneath him, the whole back of the dragon tilted and Torr clung on tightly, hoping that no one fell off. Behind him, Nattie's fingers dug sharply

ROBERT SMITHBURY
email: astro.saga.oblique.media@gmail.com

into his shoulders. A cacophony of complaining girls' voices emerging from beneath the cloak.

"What's going…"

"… on? It's dark …"

"…in here. Someone…"

"… take a look outside and …"

"…see what's happening…"

"...Oooh. This is..."

"... fantastic. We seem to be ..."

"...heading off somewhere. I ..."

"...wonder where? Another ..."

"...adventure. Whoopee ..."

"... this is the best vacation yet!"

Torr sighed heavily as their dragon aligned itself with the others and the 'formation' became apparent even to him. Whilst it was difficult to spot the other black dragons against the dark clouds, their one appeared to be flying on the extreme right of the others. To their left, slightly ahead in the general direction of flight there was a line of three dragons, each slightly in front of the other and amazingly even larger than the dragon they were flying on. There was one that was so huge that it could only be described as monstrous. Further out ahead of their own dragon were another two dragons, Torr counted, making six in all.

One of the other dragons shouted across to where Torr was flying, "That's the sort of typical shabby flying we've come to expect from you, Soot."

"Yeah," screeched another. "What Fang just said. Doubled! Who taught you to fly; a rock?"

One of the dragons ahead of them cawed a reply.

"Leave Soot alone Smasher! You just concentrate on your own flying,"

Torr leaned forwards along the dragon's neck and tried his best to whisper into his dragon's ear.

"Is that your name, Soot?"

The dragon inclined its head slightly to look at him from one smouldering eye, "Yes," it growled. "What if it is?"

"Oh nothing really. Just wondering, that's all. My name's Torr, I'm pleased to meet you."

"Likewise, I'm sure."

"I think it's a really sweet name," chirped Nattie from behind him.

"Quiet!" roared a human voice, full of annoyance and impatience from the front. "This is a combat mission. It's essential that we retain silence."

The storm immediately denied the order with a tremendous clap of thunder that bypassed his ears and made Torr's brain vibrate in angry sympathy. That voice was familiar but Torr couldn't quite place it. The echoing acoustics made it impossible for him pin it down as he struggled to concentrate on the sound. As he grappled to file away the voice's exact pitch and tone for later consideration it slyly slipped from his memory amidst the confusing cacophony of sights and sounds that assaulted his senses. Just staying in his seat on the back of a tempest-riding dragon was giving him enough to contend with.

However, despite the danger and regardless of the recklessness, he would be the first to admit that there was a bit of a thrill about it all. This was quite an adventure! How many boys got to ride a black dragon? he thought. His legs gripped the dragon's neck and shoulders, fitting easily into the riding stirrups. With each beat of the dragon's wings he could feel the powerful muscles fight against the artificial gravity of the asteroid's spin.

Far below, another volcano belched a huge cloud of ash that shot skywards forcing the flight of dragons to bank sharply. This time they perfectly maintained their highly prized formation whilst completing their manoeuvre.

How much more of this volcanic activity can the asteroid take, thought Torr, alarmed at the thought of the protective crust shattering, spilling them all into the even more hostile environment of outer space.

With mounting trepidation, Torr hung tightly onto the reigns; behind him, he could feel the others battle to avoid sliding off and plummeting to the surface far below. On all sides, Torr noticed other erupting volcanoes scattered across the landscape laid out far beneath. Each was marked out by bright sparks of winking light that seemed to be calling to him amidst the darkness of the thunderstorm.

Where were they going, he wondered?

With that thought, his mind raced forwards. Here they were riding a thunderstorm on the back of a dragon following five others flying into the unknown terrors of a violent, primeval landscape. Civilisation and the Eos were a long way behind them. So how were they going to get out of this one?

~o0o~

Somewhat closer than had previously been the case, Tina's temper was deteriorating rapidly. She could feel the telling dampness of a wet patch beneath her. The storm was making the ground tremble and she still hadn't figured out who was doing all that humming!

Grumbling, she struggled to rise from the nest and made an ungainly attempt to stand. Lowering her head close into the nest she opened her jaws and gave all of the remaining eggs one of her biggest and best earth-shattering roars. All of the eggs shook, inwards and outwards.

Now shut up that humming and go to sleep!

~oOo~

Elsewhere in the storm, but protected from the heavy weather, bright lights glinted off gaily decorated, armoured space suits.

"Target locked on deep within the Saurox Theme Park, Ma'am. Heading 20~17~58. The beacon is still stationary and giving off that very interesting energy signature. The one that resonates closely with our secret..."

"Sssshhh!"

Lady Medea's fingers drummed impatiently on the arm of the large, pink, heavily overstuffed, leather swivel chair. It occupied the prime position on the bridge of the Dragon's Storm but even it virtually disappeared amidst the vivid, over-stylised interior decoration. The chair itself was swamped by a cloud of feathers and boas that sprouted in huge colourful sprays of red, pink and white all around it. Within the arresting, avian array a cascading, multi-tiered display of flowers was intertwined, leaving a pungent fragrance circulating around the centre of the ship's bridge. Around them colourful exotic plants filled the nooks and crannies, potted in delicately decorated ceramics, anchored to every conceivable surface. Any space that wasn't filled with abundant foliage had been stuffed with an unusual collection of stuffed furry animals and assorted taxidermic paraphernalia. Heavy flock wallpaper and dark drapes covered the walls and doorways. If Nattie could have seen it she wouldn't have approved of such an arcane approach to spacecraft ornamentation.

Patience, patience, Lady Medea cautioned herself as the ship glided effortlessly across the volcanic plain. Despite the fierceness of the conditions outside it remained unaffected by the worst of the weather, its advanced technologies predicting and evading each sudden volcanic outburst.

Once she had completed her investigation of this interesting energy signature her revenge would follow swiftly afterwards. She'd quickly find those two annoying and unbelievably frustrating children who had thwarted her attack on the Santa Anna. She'd track them down to somewhere where there'd be no one to help them. Then she'd be the one who had the last laugh.

There would be no one to remember them after she had totally obliterated them, she promised herself as she slammed her fist against the padded armrest. A teacup and saucer rattled ominously in reply. No one would wonder what had become of them once she had eliminated them from history, she vowed.

Her interest in the last unusual energy source they had investigated had paid off handsomely and a combination of luck and cunning bravado may well do once again, she thought as she concentrated her attention to chasing down every opportunity for piratical profit.

"Maintain our distance!" she barked, her mind shifting back to the present. "It is essential to remain beneath the ground radar and undetected by any so-styled law enforcement agencies."

Soon, she promised herself. Very, very soon, all of her planning would come to fruition. The second energy source first and the children second. Curiosity and avarice for starters, revenge for dessert.

Chapter 11: ...into the fire

Soot and the rest of the dragon formation changed direction and started to circle. As they did so Nattie tried to get Torr's attention above the continuous clamouring from the storm.

"I think we're starting to descend."

Torr realised that she was correct, again. Now was probably the time to tell the others about the plan he had been thinking about.

"I have a plan," he said over his shoulder. "Pass it on."

"Pass what on? Having a plan is hardly news. Is it a good one?" asked Nattie.

Torr thought about that for a moment. Better to be honest.

"Probably not, but it's all we've got."

"In that case I want to hear it before I make any promises about who I might pass it onto."

"OK, I guess."

"Well?"

Torr hesitated, "I'm feeling a bit embarrassed about it now."

"If you don't tell me about it soon then its going to be academic because in a few minutes we'll all be on the ground."

"Okay, okay," Torr sighed. "Here it is," he paused, spreading his hands expansively before finding nothing in them. He felt foolish. Nattie had to nudge him from behind to continue. "Okay, well, we guide Soot in to land on one side of the formation. Then as the other riders are dismounting we climb down the other side of Soot that's hidden from them and hide nearby."

"What happens then?"

"That's as far as I got," admitted Torr weakly.

Nattie tried hard to keep her patience and spoke slowly as if to a small child.

"We're a long way from home, Torr. How are we going to get safely back to the ship?"

"I know," admitted Torr. "There are a lot of volcanoes between here and the Eos. If only there was some way that she could fly herself here?"

"Why don't we ask Kiki?" asked Nattie, trying hard not to sigh out loud.

Torr had forgotten all about Kiki who had sneaked in under the cloak and was still hiding from the storm.

"Kiki!"

"Yes boss?" came a muffled reply.

"Can the Eos fly out here on her own?"

"I'm afraid not."

Torr's heart sank.

"The volcanic eruptions have played havoc with communications. I'm out of contact with the Eos and have been for some time now."

"Oh bother! What are we going to do?"

"I've an idea, boss!"

"Well?"

"I could go back and get the Eos. Once I'm close enough to open up radio communications I can get the Eos to meet me half way."

"Are you sure? Is it safe?"

"Well, we're flying across a volcanic landscape on the back of a Draco Magnificat Necrom towards an uncertain doom that we seem to be descending directly into. From a relative perspective, anywhere that isn't here is safe."

"Good point," muttered Torr darkly. "You'd better get started. Good luck."

"Thanks, but I think you'd better hang onto that luck, boss. You're going to need all you can get. One last thing..."

"What?"

"The Fourth Secret...."

"Yes?" Torr asked. Kiki suddenly had his full attention.

"We've been flying steadily towards it for the last three hours. Wherever it is that we're going, the Fourth Celestial Secret is inextricably mixed up in it. That probably explains why the weather is so bad. The Fourth Celestial Secret must be the one that moderates the weather and volcanic activity. It's designed to stop asteroids from having unstable ecosystems and quickly becoming uninhabitable."

Torr gulped. Nothing simple then.

"The Fifth Celestial Secret is also here on Triassica as well, but I don't have such a close fix on that. All I can tell you is that it's around somewhere. Byeeeee!"

Kiki released his hold on Torr's shoulder and he disappeared as the blinding slipstream whisked him away.

"What...?" Torr called to the wind but Kiki was already long gone.

Two Celestial Secrets nearby, he mused. What difference would that make?

Behind him one of the triplets sighed, which apparently was the cue for them to start parcelling out the conversation again.

"This ride is..."

"...getting so..."

"... boring. Can we..."

"...go home..."

"...now?"

"Yes, I need..."

"...we need..." one of them insisted.

"We need..."

"...a shower and..."

"...something to eat."

Food, now there's a thought, pondered Torr. The last time he had eaten had been back at the circus before he went in search of Nattie. His stomach belched to remind him that Nattie had never returned with the hot dogs that she'd promised it. Hungrily, he stared down at the violent landscape far below them. There was no sign of food or life anywhere on the blasted terrain.

They were descending much more quickly now and the ruined ground was coming up fast. It was almost time for his plan and even he could see it was looking flimsier by the moment. The terrain was very rocky and a number of small volcanoes were still spouting acrid smoke into the stormy skies. Rain continued to lash at them and Torr was already beginning to miss Kiki. Possiwhatsit lasers would be extremely comforting right now.

"Soot?"

In reply, the dragon rumbled beneath him.

"What now?" it growled.

"Can you land us on one side of the other dragons? I'd rather that they didn't know we were here."

"Hmmmm," Soot grumbled. "I'll think about it."

The ground was now coming up sickeningly fast. Torr glanced over his shoulder at where Nattie and the triplets were still hiding underneath the cloak.

"We're coming down. Prepare yourself for a landing and you'd better get those three up to speed with what our plan is," Torr said.

"Gee thanks! Our plan? Don't you mean your plan?" Nattie's muffled voice hissed sarcastically from beneath the cloak and this time she did sigh. "Would you like me to do anymore impossible things whilst I'm at it?"

"Breakfast would be a good one," Torr grinned just seconds before the floor hit them with the explosive force of a locomotive and Soot let out a belch of caustic, sulphurous flame.

They had landed.

Dragons weren't known for their subtlety. Moments later another five thunderclaps split the air as the remaining dragons landed beside them.

Torr peeked through the slits of the dragon rider's helmet he had donned and realised that Soot had completed the first part of the plan successfully. They were over on one side of the small clearing they had landed in, part of a thin, shallow valley. Hundreds of caves in a variety of sizes and shapes dotted the cliff face next to them. Ahead, a ridge of earth had been thrown up by what looked like the burnt our remnants of a crashed spacecraft. Now it was time for the next part of his plan; getting off the dragon without attracting any attention.

"Quick. All off on this side," Torr hissed as he slipped down the dragon's enormous girth.

Around the clearing, the remaining dragon riders were also dismounting. Removing large swords from their packs and picking up shields covered in a variety of different black and white symbols, they seemed to be preparing for some kind of fight. Torr hoped it wasn't with him.

The others slid from Soot's back and landed in a jumbled heap. Torr stared around at their blackened faces from the clouds of volcanic ash they had been flying through. Even Fuzz ball looked like she'd been dipped in tar. The five of them looked at him blankly and Nattie spoke for all of them.

"Okay, what now?"

And with a sinking feeling, Torr realised there was nothing more in his plan. It was empty. This was it.

He could hear the sound of claws scrabbling on rocks nearby and he suddenly had everyone's attention.

They all looked at him with shifting expressions. He couldn't understand why. Were they looking at him, or were they looking at something behind him?

Behind him?

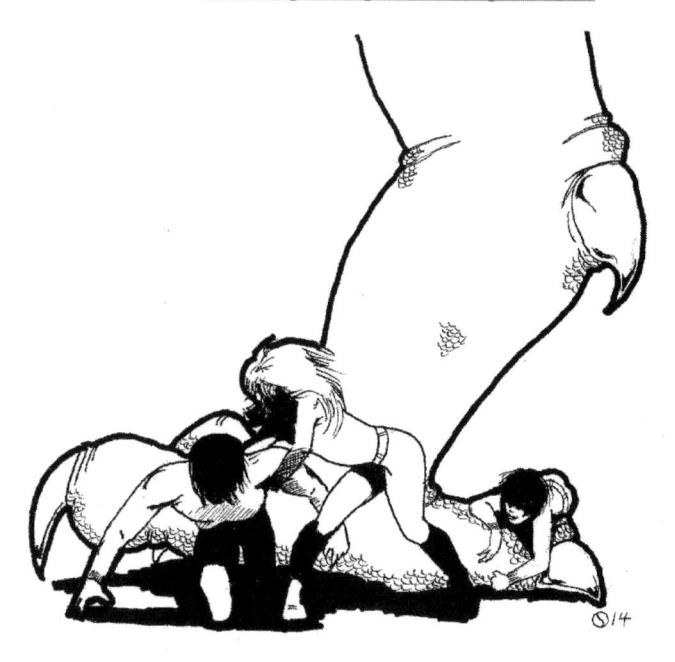

He felt a heavy movement of the air at his back. Something was stirring deep from the cave behind him.

Something big.

Something angry.

Something that hopefully wasn't as hungry as he was.

Torr could see the others starting to back away from him and his legs were already moving of their own accord before Nattie's scream reached his ears, "Run!"

He didn't even stop to look over his shoulder as the others sprinted around to the other side of Soot, mere microseconds ahead of him. He just had a terrifying urge to get as far away as possible from whatever was stirring within the cave.

In front of him Torr could hear the bellows of the black dragons as they argued amongst themselves.

He reached Soot and leapt the gradually rising crest of the dragon's tail to land in the relative sanctuary of the other side. Without looking he ran straight into the backs of the others. All of whom had inexplicably stopped dead in their retreat from the shadowy monsters from the caverns.

What now, he fumed. What could possibly make them stop running?

"Ahhh, Mr Naydo, so good of you to join us."

It was that voice from the flight again. The one he thought he had recognised shouting at them to get in formation. He stared around him to see where it was coming from. Who was it?

"Up here you fool!" the voice bellowed in irritation.

Torr's gaze followed the long line of another dragon's neck to where its diminutive rider sat triumphant waving a sword at them whilst using his other hand to pull menacingly on his dragon's reins. Monolithic memories that Torr had buried deep within the abandoned quarries of his darkest nightmares shifted uneasily. They whispered a name amongst themselves just loud enough for him to hear the sound but too quietly for him to recognise it.

Chapter 12:
If auld acquaintance be forgot...

"Who are you?" Torr shouted.

"How quickly you forget," exclaimed Lord Steal, boasting loudly over the roaring dragons. "Though no one who has heard it, ever really forgets the name of Lord Steal; First Space Lord of the Aztex Empire, destroyer of all enemies, annihilator of worlds, spectre of the space ways!"

The grinding memories in Torr's brain echoed the tyrant's words. Images of the frozen wasteland of NördStrörm, the hunter killer polar bears, the Tower of Neidelkreig, Kezin the lion boy! All of these images erupted from his memories in a surge of pent up emotion. But the overriding picture of Lord Steal disappearing into the blizzard hotly pursued by two angry, hungry, mutated polar bears that was the one recollection that he'd clung to. How was the diminutive dictator here, now?

"But ... you're dead! How did you survive?" Torr screamed in frustration, whilst a frightened Nattie clung fiercely to his arm.

Lord Steal just laughed, "I'd worry more about your own survival! Did you really expect me not to notice six of you clinging to the back of one of my own dragons? Now that you are a long way from any hope of rescue I have you completely at my mercy! Let me introduce you to your doom. Death at the hands of my black dragons!"

Lord Steal raised his arm high in triumph before swinging it around in a wide arc and pointing it directly at the children, "Fang, Smasher! Kill them, rend them limb from limb, feast on their flesh and have their bones for your breakfast."

Tara, Kara, Sara all screamed together as the two most evil looking of the black dragons turned glowing red eyes towards them before leeringly licking their lips.

"Aaaaa…"

"…aaaa…."

"….rrrrggghh!"

The triplet's screams echoed around the canyon, before a moaning, groaning, rumbling, grumbling deep throaty growl of defiance and rage started up in harmony from behind Torr. The monsters were finally emerging fully from the shadows of the cave and now no one could deny the threat they posed.

Panic peppered the air as the dragons pensively positioned themselves.

Soot's claws scrambled for a secure footing and his large, dark body reared up as he prepared to face whatever danger was finally emerging from the mouth of the caverns. His enormous tail lashed around to retain his balance as he turned to face the cave entrance, scattering the children behind him. Even Lord Steal's mount, Rip, took a couple of steps back, finding room to 'fight in', with the other dragons fanning out behind him.

Picking himself up from where Soot's tail had swept him, Torr looked wildly around for somewhere to hide from whatever it was that was going on. Kiki had said that the Fourth Celestial Secret was somehow mixed up in their destination. Between the six black dragons, Lord Steal, the soldiers and whatever was emerging from the cave mouth, he wasn't quite sure how anybody knew what was happening. He was certain that they wouldn't have the sense of mind to be looking around for small, egg shaped objects that were probably the only thing that stood between humanity and certain doom. That meant it would all be up to him. As usual.

Soot was looking around too, but not for Celestial Secrets. He was too close to the emerging threat and too far away from the other dragons for support. He couldn't retreat further without fear of trampling Torr and his friends, who remained in scattered clusters around his sturdy, stocky, legs.

"Move!" he roared at them all.

"Oh for the Death God's sake Soot, stop worrying about them and get in position," screeched Eclipse, the haughty female of the flight. "They're only humans!"

"Soot's afraid of the tiny humans," snorted Smasher before trumpeting loudly at the huge head that had eyed him hungrily from the cavern's mouth.

"Scaredy lizard!" taunted Fang as the team of riders loudly beat their swords against their shields, adding to the deafening din that echoed around the valley walls.

""Kill! Kill! Kill!" screeched Lord Steal and Rip in awful, awesome harmony as the hillside reverberated with the renewed battle cries of this new threat.

The black dragons were becoming skittish at this first sight of the dinosaurs. Their inexperience against a real enemy was beginning to undermine their confidence. Human children, lizard men, they were easy enough but gigantic dinosaurs were another story all together.

Soot's eyes caught Nattie's, "I'm sorry," he whimpered nervously. "But my loyalty must be to my hatchlings."

So saying, he turned his face away from them and faced the enemy. His long tail swished behind him he lurched backwards. Gradually Nattie and the others were being forced to retreat further towards the eager, skittish, dripping fangs of the other black dragons.

"Scatter!" screamed Nattie, pushing the triplets in one direction and Fuzz ball in the other.

Fuzz ball bounced back immediately, she wasn't leaving Nattie's side. Her furry feet scrambled furiously at the rocks and scree in an attempt to gain traction. The floor refused to stay stable beneath her and she fell forwards onto her face. The sky darkened further as dragons stomped into threatening positions and Smasher's clawed foot slammed into the ground between the girls. Rivulet's of mud splashed up everywhere, smothering them all in soft, clinging, gruesomely vile ooze that only added to their blackened sooty look.

~oOo~

"We have ground radar on the target site Ma'am. There appear to be nearly a dozen large beasts and humans all milling around in the vicinity. If I had to guess I would say there was some sort of fight going on."

"How close are they to the unique energy signature we've been tracking?"

"Within 500 metres. That's as close as I can place it."

"Put us in a holding pattern. I don't want to get too close to any battle that might be going on. We can always deal with any victor later while they're licking their wounds. Let's wait until we know a little more."

Her long nailed, claw-like fingers went back to drumming on the plush, pinkly padded arm of her chair. Patience, patience an inner voice insisted.

Damn patience, another voice replied in something resembling a mental screech. Damn her and those other children to hell!

~oOo~

A panic stricken Fuzz ball leapt onto the nearest dragon's claw before it could fly skywards again. She bounced once, twice, and landed in Nattie's arms. Almost immediately, Smasher's foot lifted high in the air before crashing down to earth again where Torr had just been standing.

Instead, he was already rolling and tumbling across the rocky floor of the valley. The whole area had become a danger zone for anything that wasn't dragon sized or possibly bigger. Without anything more calculated than running away from anything even vaguely hazardous he headed straight for the shelter of the large rocks that were scattered along the valley walls. He needed space focus on finding the Fourth Secret.

Lord Steal's voice echoed above the fighting calls of the dragons, the rain and storm, taunting Torr as he fled.

"I'll deal with you later, Naydo! There's nowhere you can hide from me. Even the Gates of Titan can't conceal you from my wrath."

He turned his dragon towards the new threat.

ROBERT SMITHBURY
email: astro.saga.oblique.media@gmail.com

Torr stared around him from the relative shelter he'd discovered at the edge of the battle arena. Soot had now retreated into the centre of the valley, withdrawing before the presence of two new behemoths that had finally emerged from the caves. The pair of Tyrannosaurs towered over the black dragons that appeared terrifyingly tiny compared to these new, awesome monsters. These prehistoric beasts had a wild and savage confidence about them as they swaggered arrogantly forwards. They showed no fear, just pure, unbridled, deadly decisiveness.

Lord Steal stared at the dinosaurs with savage appreciation. With dismay he had to admit to himself that they were far bigger than he'd expected. Why hadn't the scout reported this? His dragons were dwarves in comparison.

But he knew that size was no judge of stature and no substitute for low-down cunning. All that was in doubt was whether the dragons had the wily, weaselly, winning streak that coursed through his own veins. They had to. There was no other choice remaining.

He screamed his orders, "Kill, kill, kill! Overwhelm them with your numbers, rush them whilst you still have the element of surprise."

The black dragons stared at him incredulously. Who did this human think he was?

"There are six of you," he continued ranting at the black dragons. "You're the ultimate creation of twenty generations of gene splicing and recombination to create the most fearsome fighting beasts of legend. There's just two of these oversized clones of ancient, deficient DNA. Kill, kill, kill!" he insisted.

~oOo~

The Dragon's Storm hovered just above the surface of the volcanic plane, hidden from the valley where the black dragons were under attack behind a large basalt crag of rock.

Inside the high tech environment of the space ship patience was in short supply.

On the bridge, Lady Medea plucked the last flower from the empty bouquet surrounding her. Petal by petal she stripped it bare.

"I hate them, I hate them not, I hate them, I hate them not."

As she finished, "I hate them not!" she discarded the naked stem into the ankle deep pile of stalks and petals around her feet.

"Damn! Why don't things ever turn out like you want them to? Why is it that fate never, ever gets it right and a woman always, always has to lend a hand?!"

She glared around the bridge at the empty vases.

"...and why are we never near a florist when I need one?"

Chapter 13: A cunning plan

Torr was sheltering on one side of the valley with the overnight bag slung haphazardly across his back. After the day he'd had he wasn't about to leave it behind anywhere, ever again. On the other side of the valley was Nattie, with Fuzz ball clinging to her neck and the triplets gawking around in wide, six-eyed surprise. In between them were six black dragons, five armoured soldiers and two Tyrannosaurus Rex, which would be complication enough for most boys. But Torr had the added worrying complexity of the Fourth Celestial Secret to worry about as well.

The only good piece of news in his whole day was that the Tyrannosaurs and the black dragons appeared to be much more interested in fighting each other than in devouring Torr and his friends. No doubt, Torr thought dismally, that would change as soon as it was decided who had won. At the moment, his fate looked decidedly dicey. Whoever emerged victorious, they were in more trouble than ever before and likely to end up as someone else's supper before they saw their own.

Fiercesome lightening continued to lance across the sky but the rumbling thunder was impossible to make out above the incessant roaring of the dragons and dinosaurs. Even the ground shook erratically beneath their crashing footfalls and the rain fell in torrents, churning the once dusty earth into deep, dark, puddles of mud.

Fate looked at Destiny.

"Now?" he asked.

"Now," she confirmed.

The Tyrannosaurs had formed a defensive shield around the cave entrance and the black dragons were warily testing their strength. Fang leapt forwards to let fly with a burst of flame but the deluge of rain was dampening his biological furnace and all he could cough up was a dusty cloud of ash. As he stared in shocked confusion at what had emerged from the end of his nose, the smaller of the Tyrannosaurs caught him and sunk her teeth deep into his wing. He screamed pitifully and struggled fitfully to scrabble away from his captor.

"Smasher! Smasher! Help meeeee!" he pleaded uselessly.

Unusually shy Smasher hid even further behind Midnight, urging the large mute dragon forwards. "Kill, Midnight, kill!" he whispered urgently.

Midnight hesitated and the larger of the Tyrannosaurs seized the moment. Head down he charged at the whole flight of blacks, scattering them before him.

"Resistance is useless!" he screeched as he rampaged amongst them.

Behind him Tina roared words of encouragement.

"Scare them off Timothy, show them that they can't come and steal our eggs!"

Tina spat out the chewed remnants of one of Fang's wings with a look of distaste.

"Pfuugh! Filthy, dirty dragons shoo!"

Of course, this was all largely said in dinosaur-ease sothe overall effect was largely wasted on the scattering dragons. Fortunately, though the Tyrannosaurs actions were speaking loudly enough for everyone to understand them.

Timothy's attack had given the Tyrannosaurs the upper hand and they weren't going to waste it. In the melee of thrashing claws and teeth Timothy rumbled forwards, past the very spot where Torr was doing his best to merge into the wall.

Clinging to the wall tightly as tons of dinosaur rushed past his eyes, he suddenly realised that there was nothing between him and the empty cave mouth. It was as if the hand of fate had swept a trail clear before him. An avenue of empty space opened up in front of his eyes.

Torr stared blindly into the shadowy, darkness at the far end. But what awaited him deep inside the cave?

The lightening suddenly flashed briefly and brightly enough for him to see the concealed dinosaur eggs, nestling within a carefully constructed pile of rocks and broken bones.

Darkness crashed back again. But amidst the inky blackness and fragmented after-image, Torr felt sure that one of the eggs twinkled at him. A thrill electrified his spine. Was that the Fourth Secret?

Then, when he least expected it an ugly, ominous question crept into his ears and looked him straight between the eyes. Did the dinosaurs really think it was one of their eggs?

Oh no!

Inside Torr's head neurones fired off in all directions and then eccentrically pursued each other around his brain in parabolic orbits. A new thought was forming, struggling against his in built sense of self-preservation, reason and sanity. Madness momentarily overcame sensibility.

How could he sneak in and get his hands on the Fourth Celestial Secret without being set upon by two half-crazed, enormous, over-bred, over-protective Tyrannosaurs?

~oOo~

On board the Dragon's Storm a flurry of feathers and soft cushions had exploded under a fusillade of frustrated fists.

"I'm fed up with waiting around. I want action and I want it now!" screamed Lady Lucretia Medea at the top of her lungs.

Her patience was in shreds somewhere amongst the tattered fragments of the flower arrangements that were now scattered across the floor. Sitting next to her, the communications officer covered his ears and started weeping quietly. Why did he ever take this job?

"I want this ship in the centre of whatever's going on and I want it now!" she screamed at him shrilly.

Patience was a long forgotten virtue and unbridled revenge now stalked unchecked through the corridors of the Dragon's Storm.

Lady Medea suddenly stood upright and rigid in the centre of the bridge, her hands clasped into tiny fists of rage and her arms extended tightly by her sides. Frantically she chewed a painted, pink lip in a vain attempt to stop herself from stamping her foot in frustration.

Steam didn't come out of her ears but clouds of muddy dust did billow up from the volcanic plain surrounding the ship. The Dragon's Storm beat its ominous wings towards the raging battle.

~oOo~

Almost rigid with terror, Torr felt a nudging at his back. Cautiously he turned around, half-frightened about what he might see behind him. He breathed out heavily when he realised that there was nothing creeping up on him. It must just be his nerves, he told himself.

With worried eyes he glanced around the rest of the valley and reviewed the situation. The advantage of the narrow confines of the valley, meant that the large male T-Rex was easily holding his own against the black dragons. Only two of them could get within striking distance and their wings were useless without sufficient room to use them.

The dragons weren't used to fighting without their flames and they appeared unsure what to do. Fang was injured and Smasher was jumping up and down, making so much of a fuss that he was next to useless whilst the riders were all hiding somewhere out of sight. On the other side of the valley, Torr could see Nattie and the others sheltering in a crack that was too narrow for the smaller T-Rex to get at them. They were safe, for the time being.

He glanced again at the open path ahead of him. Venturing into a Tyrannosaurs nest was an insane notion. Wasn't it?

The nudge at his back came again. He tried to peer over his shoulder. Still no one there.

His brain returned to the more pressing problem. How was he going to get at the Fourth Celestial Secret, hidden in amongst the dinosaur eggs, without being torn to shreds or stomped into the nearest puddle? They'd be on him in seconds as soon as he broke cover.

It wasn't until the third nudge and the third nervous check over his shoulder that he realised it was the overnight bag that had been nudging him. It was still slung, sadly, over his shoulder but gave him a damp, pathetic, neglected look as his pulled it around to stare at it. He denigrated himself for being stupid and forgetful, yet again.

'Of course, the overnight bag!' he exclaimed.

He slapped himself on the head with the heel of his palm and then instantly wished he hadn't. This needed more then senseless self-blame and unnecessary gestures. It required action and the clever use of whatever he could find to help himself. The overnight bag was top of his places to start searching for assistance.

Quickly he pulled it down to the ground and ripped open the zips. He thrust both arms deep inside and rummaged around. As usual, he wondered what he might find. An atomic axe? A suit of neutronium armour? A giant inflatable T Rex? A dinosaur destroying death ray? An enormous extending arm that he could use to grab the Fourth Celestial Secret without leaving where he was hiding? The possibilities were endless.

But unnervingly the bag appeared to be completely empty.

How could it be empty? There must be something useful that it had inside!

How could it be empty when it had been nudging him to try and tell him something?

How could it be empty now, when he needed it most?

He slumped against the wall and feeling utterly defeated, he slid down it. As he did so, a small cloth cap inter woven with intricate electrical components fell out of his back pocket and landed at his feet. Dazed, he stared at it, unable to comprehend what it was and where it had come from. Then with a start he grabbed it and knocked the mud from it. The fabric responded crisply to the touch and hummed away gently, even contentedly in his hand.

It was the Hades Cap.

With a flash of inspiration, that echoed the lightening playing across the heavens, a plan came to

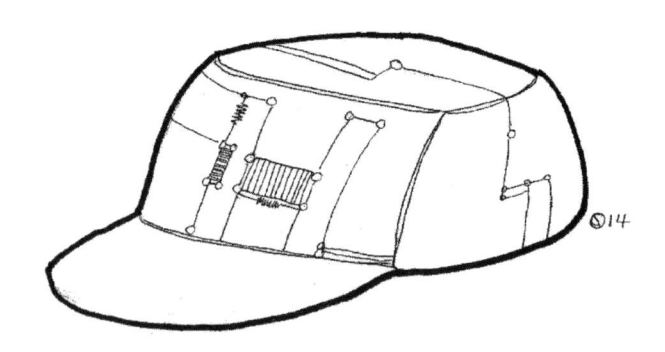

Torr. A cunning plan, a brilliant plan, a plan that just might work and would be a lot easier than inflating a giant dinosaur. The only question remaining was whether he was brave enough, or perhaps even crazy enough to try it?

He took a look at the tattered remnants of what he had once called his sanity. It was now, or never.

Chapter 14: Snatching an egg from the furnace

Torr didn't wait for his brain to catch up with what necessity had in store for him.

He gulped loudly. Torr knew that he needed to act quickly before his legs realised where they were heading and common sense kicked in.

Pulling the cap over his head, he prayed it was still working and this wasn't another of the overnight bag's tricks. Unfortunately, the laws of probability were clear that the chance of him surviving the next five minutes were significantly less than the likelihood that he'd end his days as dinner for a dinosaur. He tried to stop himself thinking about it anymore. There was no time for morbidity. The dinosaurs could turn at any moment.

Jumping out from behind the rock he'd been cowering behind, Torr started running at full pelt towards the nest of eggs. His heart was already pounding in his chest.

Behind him, the larger of the T Rex was in dinosaur to dragon combat with Midnight. Off to his left the smaller T Rex had given up trying to winkle the girls out from their hiding place in the rock face. It was now facing down Eclipse who appeared to have run out of flame and instead hissed and spat smog at the enormous behemoth facing her.

Torr wasn't sure but he thought he caught sight of a small hand waving at him from a fissure in the rock face opposite. He hoped that was a promising sign and not an indication of some new problem.

Crunch! Crack! Splinter!

With shock, Torr stopped and stared down at his feet. The valley floor was littered with rocks, bones and he didn't dare guess what else. He could either pick his way gingerly between the debris, or... he hesitated to even say it out loud in his brain. Or... he could try and rush through, hoping all the while that the sound of the enormous battle and accompanying storm would drown the sound of him splashing through the puddles, crunchy bones and scattering rocks.

On the other hand, if he picked his way through quietly then he would still be carefully edging his way forwards next week. There was nothing for it but to take his chances and make a dash for it.

Without waiting for his common sense to wake up and stop him dead in his tracks he set his sights on the nest and started running. By his reckoning it was about 50 paces. His brain started counting each step as his legs pounded as fast as he could move them.

Forty five

Crunch, crack, splash

Forty four

Splatter

Forty three, was he getting any closer?

Creak, groan and another splash

Thirty nine

Crackle

Thirty eight, yes closer now.

Thirty one

Crunch

Thirty, nearly half way

Twenty six,

Splinter

Twenty five

Half way, yes definitely half way. Probably.

Twenty four. Could he feel eyes watching him? Were they friendly or silurian?

Twenty three

Crash, crunch

Twenty two

Splash. Boom

Twenty one, was that a noise behind him?

Twenty

Sniff

Nineteen. Was that a sniff?

Eighteen. Had it gone quiet? He couldn't tell. All he could hear was the noise of his own heart trying to escape from his ribcage and hide behind a rock.

Boom

Fifteen, he could feel another vibration in the air, beneath his feet, all around him.

Boom

Fourteen, there it was again, like a heartbeat in the ground.

Boom

Thirteen, another heartbeat, heavier this time.

Boom

Twelve, and again. What was going on?

Wuff, boom

Eleven and the ground breathed hard upon his neck.

The ground breathed hard upon his neck? What was going on? He dared not looked around. With an enormous effort he kept his focus on running.

Snuff, snuff

Ten and something sniffed hard upon his collar.

Terror tore at Torr's guts.

Snuffle

Nine, sniffed? Something definitely sniffed.

Torr's lungs filled with fear and self-preservation. His sixth sense pulled hard on the brakes and he skidded the last short distance into the nest. Totally out of control he barrelled into the fragile bundle of eggs.

They scattered everywhere, cracking as they did, spilling the squealing, squeaking, screeching, gurgling, baby dinosaurs out onto the floor. Egg yoke covered shards smeared themselves all over him as the tiny monsters struggled to take their first steps.

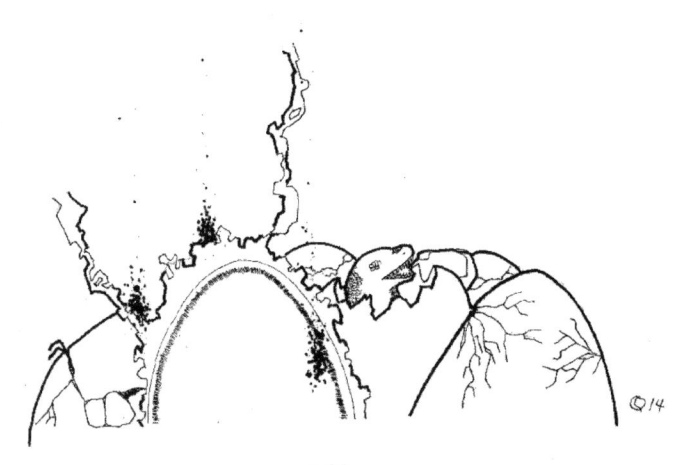

But there was one, just one egg that didn't break. The Fourth Celestial Secret! He'd been right. It was here, hidden amongst the shards of broken dinosaur eggs.

The parents must have thought the alien container was one of their own eggs and been waiting for it to hatch. Silly creatures, thought Torr as he was jostled by the babies. No wonder they'd all become extinct.

~oOo~

Tina the dinosaur stared down at the wrecked remnants of her nest. The scent of a human behind her had made her realise that she'd neglected her motherly duties and left her eggs unguarded. Hurrying back she realised that she'd been right. The nest had been under attack.

But now that her babies were hatched, their piercing cries tugged at her maternal heartstrings and her thoughts were dragged unbidden towards overriding concerns for their safety. No scent of a human remained; only empty egg and new born gunk. The remaining unbroken egg sat still, cold and lifeless.

Not worth sitting on that one, she thought, it was never going to hatch. She sighed loudly and long. Despite the urgent bleatings of her new borns she pined for the loss of her egg and berated herself for being such a bad, uncaring, mother.

A tinge of anger and blame surfaced in her consciousness and consumed her feelings of guilt. Someone was going to pay for this. Someone was going to get it big time. Some dragon was in for it!

She turned in a rage and her roar drowned out the retreating thunder. Someone was going to really regret making her angry, She headed back out into the valley, looking for trouble.

~oOo~

Torr watched in disbelief as the dinosaur that had been charging after him, sniffed carefully all over him and then turned and walked away. Couldn't she smell him? Did dinosaurs have no sense of smell? He was sure that he had had it that time. Egg yoke oozed all over him and eggshell cracked underneath his feet as he gingerly carried the Fourth Celestial Secret through the crowd of squealing dinosaur chicks. Easing through the cave mouth he slipped quietly out into the tight confines of the valley.

Ahead, the ferocious charge of the smaller dinosaur appeared to have carried the day and the black dragons were in full flight. Most of the foot soldiers had been trampled underfoot or used as mini knuckle-dusters. Soot had fled, along with Smasher. Between them they carried the heavily injured Fang. Rip had retired early after dumping Lord Steal upside down in the mud as soon as his false bravado, bluff and bluster had been broken. Midnight was hesitating near the end of the valley, but he looked beaten as well.

Only Eclipse remained, hissing a last defiant challenge to the pair of T-Rex. In one of her claws she held a tiny, diminutive, figure up by its feet. She screeched angrily at it.

"I could feed you to these monsters. You won't make much of a meal, but you should give me time to escape. Or, I could take you for myself. You should stave off starvation for a while."

She licked her reptilian lips with a long, slimy, forked tongue.

"Nooo!" screamed Lord Steal as he dangled from her claws. "I am Lord Steal, First Space Lord of the Aztex Empire, destroyer of our enemies, annihilator of worlds, spectre of …"

"Oh shut up!" roared Eclipse. "Why don't you ever shut up? Why does supper always want to make so much noise?"

~oOo~

Aboard the Dragon's Storm everyone was on high alert and listening out for the stern instruction of their commander. There was no room for confusion or misinterpretation here.

"The entrance to the valley is just up ahead, Ma'am," reported the navigator.

"Then take us in, you fool!" she sneered anxiously in reply.

"Yes, Ma'am!"

"...and while you're at it, you'd better prepare the ultimate weapon. I expect that we might need it."

There was a hint of glee in her voice.

The weapon master's face split into an echoing grin of anticipation, "You mean the Celestial's Secret Weapon?"

"Yes," she scoffed. "But if I told everyone it was a secret then it wouldn't be a very secret, secret, would it?"

"Yes Ma'am!" replied the justly reprimanded weapons master. But inside he was elated. It wasn't everyday that you get to try out a secret weapon, especially a Celestial one.

The Dragon's Storm banked its wings sharply to avoid the edges of the steep valley. Its engines roared with the extra effort, creating an almost solid wall of noise that barrelled down the canyon as it edged carefully forwards through the narrow confines. If it was possible to be louder than the fury of the thunderstorm combined with the residual violence of the battle, then the noise of the Dragon's Storm's engines achieved it.

Further down in the valley, the sudden crescendo of sound created pandemonium. Any dragon remaining in the vicinity that could still fly took to the skies and the T-Rex scampered back into their cave, nearly trampling the invisible Torr in the process. From there, they roared their defiance, gathering chicks around them, ready to face this new dragon threat, that was even larger than they were.

As Torr had correctly surmised, whilst they were big, intelligence was one of their weaknesses.

At the sight of their return Torr quickly hid. Now, only an arm's length from his hiding place he gripped the Celestial Secret tightly to his chest.

Around him, the storm unbelievingly intensified. The blaze of lightening was almost continuous with individual balls of rampaging electricity fizzling along the sides of the ravine.

Surface rainfall streamed down the walls of the valley creating free flowing waterfalls that disappeared amidst the torrents of rain.

Against the urging of nearly every fibre in his body, Torr kept moving, edging himself further along the canyon wall. Reaching the crack where the others were still hiding he called out to them over the chaos of noise that surrounded them.

"Nattie, all of you, come on! We need to get out of here," he urged them.

"Who said that. Who's there?" Nattie queried cautiously.

Torr pulled off the cap with one hand, "It's me, now come on. I've got the Fourth Celestial Secret. We need to leave, right now. Somehow."

He glanced up and then back towards the approaching Dragon's Storm. "Somehow we need to climb our way out of this gorge."

"Whooyee!" the triplets all screamed together before starting to share the conversation around again.

"What happened..."

"... to you? Yes..."

"...you're covered in..."

"...gooey gunk and you..." they all started poking him. Totally unnecessarily in his opinion.

"...stink of omelettes!"

"Torr, we'll never make it. Look!" cried Nattie, with more than a hint of panic in her voice.

Torr knew without looking that Nattie was pointing towards the unmistakable shape of the Dragon's Storm which he'd already noticed creeping towards them. He wanted to say, never mind, they could still make it but he knew that wasn't true. Whilst the rocky face of the cliff was climbable, it would still take them several hours to get to the top in this weather and what would they do when they got there? Where could they run to now?

Chapter 15: Falling

Inexplicably a rope ladder dropped in front of Torr's face. Without thinking he grabbed Nattie's arm and wrapped her frozen fingers around the rungs. The rope was cold, wet and rough.

"Climb!" he shouted at her over the noise of the thunder, before grabbing the next cold, wet limb that poked from the sheltering crack in the rock.

Whilst he had his suspicions, he didn't *know* where the rope ladder led, but anywhere was better than where he was right now.

"Wow! What…"

"… a show. That…"

"… really was the best…" the triplets chattered away, passing the conversation up and down the ladder as they climbed skywards.

"… bit of the whole…"

"… trip. I'm so…"

"… glad that Mum…"

"… and Dad paid…"

"… out for this holiday."

Holiday? thought Torr. Holiday? What were they, mad? And what was it with this continuation of their sentences. What were they, clones of each other?

Did they just have the one brain, but three bodies, and worst of all, three mouths? Couldn't there just be one of them? In what possible way did the Universe benefit from there being three of them? Weren't two redundant?

Through the rain he could just make out the horrifying head of the Dragon's Storm with its giant gaping dragon's jaws progressing inexorably down the valley towards him. Grabbing another arm, he pulled the last of the triplets from the rock face and pushed her at the ladder.

As soon as she (Torr still couldn't tell one from the other) cleared the bottom rungs of the ladder, he grabbed hold himself.

"Okay Kiki, take her away."

With a sudden lurch, he was wrenched skywards. His hunch had been right. It was Kiki with the Eos.

"We are on a heading towards deep space at optimum velocity. We have forty five seconds until we reach the asteroid lock," announced a voice that was at times annoying, but was currently doing a good impression of the best sound in the solar system. "You need to be on this side of the air lock by the time we hit space. Please take a tight hold as I'm about to start reeling in the ladder."

"Kiki, stop!"

The Eos screeched to a halt, leaving him swinging at the end of an extremely long pendulum. In a nightmare moment that stretched away into infinity he swung through the storm.

"Noooo! I don't mean stop, stop," Torr shouted in frustration and the Eos began accelerating again. "I mean 'Hang on a minute, we're forgetting the Fifth Celestial Secret'. Before you disappeared you said that the Fifth Celestial Secrets was also nearby. I've got the Fourth Celestial Secret, but the Fifth is still around here somewhere. We can't leave it behind. But don't stop here. The Dragon's Storm will …"

The power winch yanked him through the Eos' air lock and the doors slammed shut behind him.

Dragging himself across the floor, he rolled the Fourth Celestial Secret towards Nattie.

"Quick, put it in the microwave, I mean the transportamatic! If the Tinkerer can fix the Fourth Celestial Secret then at least this storm will stop."

Despite the danger, Nattie managed a half smile. The microwave doubled as a matter transporter system to the Tinkerer's base in orbit around the moon. It always made her giggle as silly things have a tendency to do. The Tinkerer was their only hope of fixing the Fourth Celestial Secret before the delicate internal dynamics of the asteroids in general and Triassica specifically tore themselves apart. The violent storms and volcanic eruptions that were troubling Triassica were symptomatic of the damage that had already been done. There was only so much stress that an asteroid could take before it burst open like an over ripe banana.

Urgently, she wrestled the Fourth Celestial Secret inside and slammed the door shut, before hitting the send button.

"Oh dear," squawked Kiki. "Oh dear, oh dear, of dear!"

"Help!" screamed Nattie as the floor tilted, just when Torr reached her side.

"W..."

"...h..."

"...at?" gurgled the triplets.

"I'm registering a huge gravitational swing," brooded Kiki in a voice that sounded uncharacteristically worried and concerned. "Looks like someone has figured out how to trigger the Fifth Celestial Secret."

"I've changed my mind, it's too dangerous to stay around," shouted Torr as the 'floor' of the Eos jolted again. "Let's get into the safety of deep space where we can figure out a plan without us all getting killed."

"Too late. The gravitational well is expanding exponentially," whined Kiki with an exceptionally obvious lack of confidence and bravado. "Even the Neutrino drives can't out distance a black hole."

"A black hole?" gurgled Torr as fear ripped at his sense of success.

The words had a chilling effect on him, freezing his brain and numbing his thoughts. It was a black hole that the Tinkerer had told him had been responsible for taking his parents from him. The very words filled him with all consuming and disabling dread. If a black hole had defeated his parents then how was he expected to overcome one?

From the bridge of the Dragon's Storm, Lady Medea shrieked with laughter as she watched the Eos quiver in the clearing sky, its engines ablaze with power, but going nowhere. This was nearly too much fun, even for her. To find those annoying children here, probably with the Celestial Secret was a perfect added bonus. Now she could relish a double victory.

She flicked a powdered, pink, carefully manicured finger at the weapons master. In response, sterile, cold fingers clicked the dial around another notch and the gravitational pull on the Eos doubled again.

You could almost hear the fabricated infrastructure of the strange spaceship groan as it was torn between the inescapable pull of the captive black

ROBERT SMITHBURY
email: astro.saga.oblique.media@gmail.com

hole and the unstoppable thrust of its Neutrino engines. But the battle was already over, the unbelievably powerful thrust of the Eos' engines was as nothing compared to the power of the black hole held captive by the Fifth Celestial Secret and wielded unmercilessly by the crew of the Dragon's Storm.

The Eos was already losing altitude, falling from the sky. Her descent accelerated further until she crashed to the ground in an ear splitting explosion of metal and dirt. Pieces of the doomed spaceship were flung across the plateau before the over heated engines exploded in a horrific fireball that rocketed across the heavens.

The weapon's technician reigned back on the dial and the captive black hole returned to dormancy under the guidance of the Fifth Celestial Secret. The triumphant Dragon's Storm stalked the wreckage for signs of life and finding none it landed safely over to one side of the plateau.

Lady Medea was beside herself with overwhelming glee as she rushed to the exit. She wanted to be the first to stride across the field of wreckage. She knew what she was looking for.

There was no sign of it anywhere, only broken metal wreckage, strewn clothes and an old battered bag. With a careless prod of her toe, she pushed at the bag. There appeared to be a box inside. Kneeling gingerly in the mud she opened the zip with a delicately gloved hand. Did the box contain what she was looking for?

No, she cursed, throwing aside the dented microwave unit that was the only item inside.

A voice spoke to her from inside her headset, "The energy signature we were following has disappeared."

Clearly, the Celestial Secret hadn't survived the crash. She gazed across the horizon for survivors, but for as far as she could see there was no sign of life amongst the wreckage. All that was left of the once proud spaceship was a sad, littered graveyard.

"Victory!" she gloated, burying her deep and bitter disappointment beneath a sugary coating of vengeance. Her hideous laugh crackled across the wrecked landscape.

"...and even better when mixed into a heady cocktail of revenge."

Possibly continued in the Fifth Secret?

email: astro.saga.oblique.media@gmail.com

I always love to hear what readers thought about my books so I can continue to write better ones. If you can leave a review where you purchased this, or drop me an email at

astro.saga.oblique.media@gmail.com

I would be really pleased to hear whatever you have to say.

Many thanks

Robert

Robert Smithbury

Printed in Great Britain
by Amazon